Walk East on on Burnside

Ronald Turco

By
Ronald Turco

1st Edition
2000

Imago Books
PO Box 25097
Portland, OR 97298

ISBN 0-9700131-0-8

Imago Books
PO Box 25097
Portland, OR 97298

Acknowledgments

Webster's dictionary defines fiction as 'something invented by imagination or feigned...an invented story'. Perhaps a feuilleton. This book therefore is a work of fiction. I mean who could possibly believe that there existed in Portland, Oregon, of all places, an international intrigue, an organized conspiracy of planned murders and, most of all, an attorney who develops an attraction for his secretary. The names in this story have been changed to protect the guilty. Any resemblance to circumstances or people living or, for the most part, dead is purely coincidental. Honest.

I would like to thank Joanne for reading the manuscript without comment and thus allowing me to write this the way I wanted to. I especially thank Police Chief David Bishop for his continued support of my role as homicide detective with the Beaverton Police Department. I thank Victor Calzaretta, attorney at law, for, as they say in certain circles, 'sanitizing the contents', and I thank Louie, my Chow Chow for reviewing the material and barking his approval. He has the last word. I thank my parents, Luigi and Antonetta, for teaching me that in the last analysis life is a matter of honor.

Most of all I thank my editor, Darlene Dube'. Without her organizational skills this book would not have been possible. I am honored to call her my friend.

If this book creates any problems for my contemporaries, I disavow any involvement. In fact I can't remember writing this book. I simply can't remember.

For

Mom
Pop
Millie
Lizzy
Lizon
Louie
Jimmy
Frankie
Salvy
Johnny

With thanks and appreciation, for your inspiration:
The men of the
4th Marine Division
382nd Platoon
USMC

About the Author

Ronald Turco, M.D., a former Air Force officer, has led a double life as a practicing psychiatrist and homicide detective for the past 27 years.

Dr. Turco has been instrumental in the apprehension of three serial killers and a large number of homicide perpetrators.

A Northwest author who has led many lives, he has written more than 100 essays and technical papers and five books. He received the Milton Erickson Prize for Scientific writing in 1991 and is the author of the widely acclaimed "Closely Watched Shadows", his personal account of the investigation and apprehension of a child serial killer.

He serves as Chairman of the Study Group on Art and Creativity of the American Academy of Psychoanalysis

An incurable adventurer, he lives with his wife, Joanne, and Chow Chow, Louie, in Portland.

Preface

On a dark rainy night in the City of Roses the blood soaked bodies of two Asian males were strewn like pieces of garbage. A short distance away a scenario of murder and intrigue unfolded. Before the night was over there would be more, dead.

"Unit 476-Code 4. Officer down...Broadway and...correction. Good Samaritan Hospital. Officer down. Unit 519-homicide! Request secure area. Apartment house at 641 Couch. Asian male, approximately 45. Throat slashed. Second Asian male three blocks south. Apparent suicide-possible homicide. Possible related. Unit 518 double shooting - possible homicide. Asian Gate - entrance to Chinatown. Backup requested for all units. Repeat backup for all units."

She walks in beauty, like the night
  Of cloudless climes and starry skies;
And all that's best of dark and bright
Meet in her aspect and her eyes:
Thus mellowed to that tender light
  Which heaven to gaudy day denies.

Lord Byron

ONE

GRETA

She was stunning! Absolutely stunning. Tall, slender, aquiline eyes - deep set - and high cheekbones. Her blonde hair was neatly fastened and interlaced in a bun secured with a blue and silver latchet - understated. White blouse, single strand of pearls and blue striped skirt - medium length. White, low-heeled shoes garnished with a single small blue diagonal band. A single small gold ring on her right forefinger. His eyes were transfixed in the azure depth of hers, absorbing her beauty like a sponge. This was the kind of woman you want to grab and touch all over and hug and kiss and kiss until your face hurts.

More than sexual arousal, this chimerical visage resonated with something deep within him. He sensed a painful, haunting about himself as if there were an echo in his body. Psychiatrists call this resonance the unconscious-mystics, karma.

Like any sensitive woman she knew the effect she had on men. Men could be such children.

As she stood in the doorway of his law office, her eyes dilated. "Good morning, I'm Greta Teufel. I have an appointment with Mr. Knox at 10 AM. I'm a little early."

"I know," Jason responded. "I mean, er...ah..."

Regaining his composure as lawyers do he motioned her to the leather chair in the inner office.

"I'm Jason Knox, happy to meet you. Sorry I don't have any coffee to offer..."

Before he could finish the sentence she chimed in. "No, problem Mr. Knox, I've had breakfast already."

He was all over the place-beside himself with racing thoughts. "Please call me "Skip," after all this is Portland, Oregon not New York City.

"O.K. "Skip."

Larry Gelb, her divorce attorney, had referred Greta Teufel to him. She had been married to a prominent cardiovascular surgeon who was all work and no play. At least no play with her. Jason thought: "My God, how could any normal, rational man overlook this woman." Her husband, according to Larry, had something of a reputation and Greta's friends referred to him as the 'D minus husband'. Larry knew Jason was looking for a good secretary. True, Greta did not have many legal skills, but she was intelligent and non-intrusive. Just the kind of woman Jason could get along with. And she was strong enough to stand up to him if necessary. Greta was Pennsylvania Dutch from Lancaster and in her mid-   forties. Mature, worldly and direct. She also knew men the way only sophisticated women know them. Neither demeaning nor condescending about relationships, she   accepted what was.

Jason did not like meddling females, a term he liked to use about some of the women legal assistants he had worked with, and he didn't like to be doted on. He was a lousy cook but preferred breaded down meatloaf to fussy dishes served with even more fuss. Much of the

4

time he preferred his own company and the silence of an occasional fishing buddy. His reputation in the legal community was as an easygoing competent lawyer and both plaintiffs and defense attorneys respected him. He was always invited to the law office parties and socials but seldom went, preferring to drink red wine alone and take in the broad vista of the Willamette River from the deck of his condo.

"Here is my resume and some references. I have more if need be."

She was laconic and precise. The lawyer in Jason liked that.

"Thank you. I already know a little about you and it won't take too long for me to look these over. Larry, er, Mr. Gelb mentioned that you speak some languages."

"Yes, German and Spanish. I know a little Italian but can't read it. I guess you could say I'm fluent in Spanish."

With the expanding Hispanic population in the Portland area Jason knew this would be an important asset. Even police departments in the State were looking for bilingual officers.

"Well that's really helpful. I'm not much with languages myself."

She appreciated his self-effacement. This was a man who could admit to shortcomings. Greta just nodded.

Jason didn't understand why she wanted the job, as Greta Teufel certainly didn't need the money. Her divorce settlement left her with plenty, including a house in Central Oregon. He thought it might be at Black Butte Ranch. Lawyers gossip and Larry had told Jason plenty. He was taken with her himself and careful to never mention this client to his jealous wife. Maybe, just maybe, the referral to Jason was a secret way to keep in touch with her or at least to hear about her.

Later Jason learned that Greta's parents had lived in Lancaster, Pennsylvania and her father worked as a successful bank executive for the Philadelphia Savings Fund Society, commuting from Lancaster to Philadelphia a few times a week. He had been instrumental in raising foreign capital, especially in Germany and Portugal and so the family traveled together when the children were out of school. Both Greta and her older brother had attended the prestigious Andrews Academy in Williamsport, Pennsylvania. Her older brother followed his father in banking, eventually landing a job in Graz, Austria in support of the American industries seeking to make inroads in that country. Greta went on to Mt. Holyoke College in Massachusetts graduating with a degree in English and a minor in foreign language. She worked in Boston for a time and met her husband during his first year of surgery residency at Boston Hospital. He wanted no children.

Greta Teufel was indeed an offer Jason could not refuse.

"Well, I see you prefer to work in a quiet office as your main goal."

"Yes, Mr. Knox, 'Skip'. I'm basically looking for something interesting to do without the confusion of lots of people and pressure. I know lawyers have deadlines and schedules but I'm good with detail and keep track of things well. Organization is one of my assets. I learned that from my father. He's retiring and my parents are moving to Central Oregon. They fell in love with the area when they came out to visit on vacation."

Greta avoided mentioning her X's name.

"So, this is another reason I want to stay in the area. I am, also, taking some night classes at PNCA."

"PNCA?" Jason interjected.

"Yes, Pacific Northwest College of Art. I work in oils but have a special interest in tempera. After all I'm from Pennsylvania."

Jason didn't get the connection but thought best to let it go. Enough questions for one day. Besides, he felt tired. He had been so in tuned with this interview that he almost forgot about a 10:30 deposition he was supposed to take. In fact he had forgotten what day it was.

"Well, that sounds great. Here are some notes I made on salary and benefits, vacation days and health insurance."

Greta studied the handwritten notes made on yellow legal paper. "I had some idea of this before I came in and it looks fine."

"Oh," Jason responded, a little surprised.

"Mr. Gelb gave me a pretty good idea of what to expect and I also had a chance to read your ad in the Bar Association Journal."

"Well, I'd love to have you work here, I mean I think you'd be happy here. When can you start?"

"Actually I could start today but I'd prefer tomorrow if that's O.K. I promised mother I'd make some calls to real estate agents and set up appointments for her and dad."

"That's fine. Tomorrow at 9 then? I'll set out some files and make some notes to orient you to my current cases and what needs first priority."

Jason had been in law practice for five years and this was his first secretary-legal assistant. That he was excited would be characterized as an understatement.

"See you tomorrow."

"Bye now."

He watched her, gawked at her, as she left the

office. It took some time for Jason Knox, attorney at law to calm down. Perhaps he had a sense that his life was to change dramatically.

It had been almost sixteen years ago that Jason had decided he wanted a quiet, normal kind of life. He had come to Portland as a CIA consultant and decided to stay.

Years later Jason was not surprised to read an article, in the Oregonian, written by Steve Jenning and Bill Keller, titled "University of Oregon researchers get CIA funds for project", announcing a 10 year research position relating to non verbal communications.

Accepted for the CIA grant to study deception at the Oregon Health Sciences University, then known as the Oregon Medical School, through the Department of Psychology. Jason served as the liaison consultant for the CIA.

At the same time, quite by accident, he consulted with the U.S. Secret Service on an issue regarding the Kennedy assassination.

Jason was an ardent history buff with a special interest in Lincoln. Not just the Civil War battles but Lincoln's character and legal decisions. He was fascinated as to how this seemingly simple man could make such complex and challenging legal and later Presidential decisions-standing alone and bearing the scorn of political rivals. He compared Felix Frankfurter his legal 'hero' to Lincoln.

The idea of Presidential assassinations occupied some of his study and collaboration with a social scientist led to a monograph on the subject.

It was during this time that Jason purchased documents pertaining to the Kennedy saga. Documents obtained from unnamed sources at a price. The *Kennedy*

Cabal was such a document detailing, as it did, the alleged 'plot' by a Swiss based Cabal.

Too hot to handle, Jason contacted Larry Phillips of the Secret Service and, together, some decisions were made about the brief and the material was passed on to Washington.

Things like this were almost always happening to Jason. Drama and intrigue had become a way of life and he had lived several ordinary and some extraordinary lives. His Asian exposure had rubbed off some and he frequently thought of reincarnation and the connecting links between Lincoln, perhaps Kennedy and most certainly Frankfurter. That was his way of making some sense of the world.

At any rate, when the CIA contract ended he decided to stay in Portland, having made quite a few friends in the community. He enjoyed the fishing, the mountains and the coastal resorts, if one could call them that.

The senior Mr. Kolb of Kolb, Alder and Rubenstein took him under his wing. He admired Jason's interest in family law and his desire to help people. He also recognized his acute sense of judgment and penchant for scholarship. Kolb knew some of Jason's law professors and, although he didn't share some of his political views, he adored Frankfurter.

Jason worked for a brief time with the law firm with an understanding from the start that he would not stay but that he would have his start and perhaps, just perhaps, take some clients with him when he left.

The association was mutually beneficial since the law firm had Asian clients and Jason was familiar with the ins and outs of doing business with Koreans and Japanese.

When he started out in his own law practice he took, with the senior partners blessing, the prestigious *Letni* account and various smaller accounts dealing mostly

9

with labor law. There was also a smattering of workers compensation cases, which he very selectively weeded out from what he called the "whinny crybabies" to the more seriously grieved clients. These cases frequently brought him into contact with some of the local psychiatrists.

During his tenure with the Kolb law firm Jason had also taken some advanced estate-planning courses and considered eventually building a practice in this area. He did not, yet, consider himself to be well enough qualified to obtain the necessary credentials to establish himself as an expert. The laws in this field were constantly changing and he knew that a simple mistake could resonate through time.

He loved the law - the theory and the practice. He saw in *the law* a codified basis for human behavior - for justice in its truest sense. A code to govern the behavior of humans. An extension of an all-powerful sense of unity and purpose in the universe. Perhaps an extension of the Deity: 'we hold these truths to be self-evident. That all men are created equal. That they are endowed by their *creator...*'

Frankfurter's book on the Sacco and Vanzetti case had become his bible. His work in labor law throughout 1917 had made a lasting impression on Jason. This is what America was about! Frankfurters letter to FDR in 1937 discussed how the Constitution is 'judicially' construed and he wrote of the lurid demonstration - "of the relation of men to the 'meaning' of the Constitution".

Jason had written a "special thesis" in law school on Louis Brandeis' advocacy of the Sherman and Clayton Acts. No doubt these legal philosophies would follow him if he chose to pursue the bench. For now he was more than content with his law practice and his moderate lifestyle. He sought his books, a few intimate friends and fishing.

Jason raced to the deposition and faced an inimical opposing counsel.

Someday he hoped he would be doing tax law and estate planning with a minimum of legal fighting.

He was tired but decided to head back to the office to set out some work and instructions for Greta who would be starting work the following morning.

Driving along the Beaverton-Hillsdale Highway he noticed the old Godfathers Pizza place, now a trendy luncheon stop. When CIA agents visited Portland he took them to the Godfathers and they would all sit around eating Italian submarines and drinking red wine under the watchful eyes of 'The Godfather' - a huge portrait of Marlen Brando that hung over the bar. Now he couldn't help but smile at the irony of it all.

Reaching the office building he parked along the street intending to be only a few minutes.

Jason's office was on the third floor of the downtown office building on Morrison Street, known as The Galleria, an upscale shopping and business center unlike the garish malls that have sprung up in different parts of the country. The Galleria was developed by a prominent Japanese-American who had the foresight to plan and use available space in strategic places in Portland. Politicians and business people alike sought his advice on a variety of community projects. That Jason had chosen this building to work in reflected his international, as well as community, interests and sense of local history.

Jason took the elevator and walked slowly. Fatigue was setting in but he always followed through with what needed to be done. He followed the Air Force dictum: 'The day of preparation has passed when the hour

11

of need has arrived'.

The office consisted of a waiting room and reception area, a few soft chairs and an embroidered bench, which had been a gift from a grateful client. A large palm in a wicker basket stood in one corner and various plants stood atop a bookshelf. The books were heavy duty-*Time Detectives* by Brian Fagan, *Marie Curie,* by Susan Quinn, *Thucydides-The History of the Peloponnesian War,* edited by Sir Richard Livingstone, some history books and a substantial array of the Folger Shakespeare series. There were also some magazines on a makeshift coffee table-*The New Yorker, Scientific American,* some old copies of *Realite* and *The Smithsonian* and an up to date copy of *The Wall Street Journal.* He had had a subscription to *National Geographic* but they were too beautiful to throw out and had been piled up, all over the place, so he canceled it. As it was the place was cluttered. He did have one copy stuffed in the desk drawer, a copy from December 1979 that discussed Seoul as having become a Korean showcase.

Both the office entrance door and the door to his inner office were solid oak. Jason liked privacy when he was talking to anyone. The front office door was unadorned save for a plaque: "Jason Knox, Attorney At Law." The inner office door was stained an oak color matching the muted, tastefully designed, wallpaper.

His inner office contained an oversized desk with a few notebooks and papers to one side, an intercom phone and a soft colored matching chair. He faced his clients who could be seated in soft leather chairs. Lighting was indirect from the ceiling and the walls were simply adorned. The ever-present woodcut of Lincoln was prominent, a few diplomas, his Oregon State Admission to Practice Law and a business license certificate. The only real photograph was of St. Basel's Cathedral, which Jason had taken on his last trip to Moscow. It was complex and colorful and reminded him of all that was good about the Soviet Union. Noticeably absent were any personal or family photographs.

Jason arranged some notes that needed typing in the morning. He would not have to send them out to an agency any longer. What a relief this would be.

One case involved a private airplane crash, which had occurred in Idaho. He was co-counsel as the family was bringing suit in Oregon. A labor relations brief had to be prepared. He had dictated this more than a week ago and it sat in a plastic container along with a few other tapes containing dictated letters. There was also a wrongful termination suit he was handling and possibly a divorce settlement, although he usually referred the domestic work to Larry.

Jason carefully handwrote out some instructions for Greta and set them, along with the papers and tapes, on the desk. Now, *her* desk.

He didn't allow himself to fully acknowledge it but it would be nice to have a woman around.

The drive to his condo was brief. There wasn't much traffic. He pulled into the garage and took the elevator up.

Jason found half of a tuna sandwich and some pickles in the fridge. He grabbed them along with a half filled bottle of red wine and sat in front of a large view window overlooking the river. Grabbing the remote he tuned in to CNN.

Within ten minutes he was fast asleep.

The man that hath no music in himself,
nor is not move'd with concourse of sweet sounds,
Is fit for treasons, stratagems, and spoils.

Shakespeare
The Merchant of Venice V,1

TWO

DIETER

Jason felt like hell when he woke up. He boiled some water for instant coffee, ignored the rising sun and specter of beauty that was all around his glass partitioned habitat and dressed - perfunctorily and mechanically. He slurped his coffee and left.

Reaching the office, Jason could see light inside the office.

Greta was at *her* desk talking on the telephone. Setting down the receiver as Jason walked in, she smiled and crisply and cheerfully said: "Good morning!" - It was blurted out as if she had done this every day in the same place at the same time for the last five or so years.

Jason halted in his tracks as if remembering some ancient truth.

"Hi, how on earth did you get in? I forgot to give you the key."

"Oh, I, ugh...I talked with the building superintendent. He said I didn't look like a Watergate burglar or a terrorist so he let me in and helped orient me a little to the building."

Jason was subliminally aware that Greta was wearing a saphenous blouse with what appeared to be a maroon trimmed and laced bra underneath. She was neatly coifed, sported a thin gold bracelet on her left wrist and radiated a temperate bouquet of what must most likely be French perfume. Her smile and enthusiasm were infectious.

"Oh! That's really nice. I didn't know Theo was in this early. Anyway it's good to see you. I mean I'm glad you're here..."

"I straightened up a bit, put a few things in order and looked over your notes. It is very helpful that you don't write like a doctor. Your handwriting has an esthetic style."

Jason was pleased with the compliment. It took him back a bit. *She* looked so elegant.

"Oh, by the way, Mr. Alexander called from the *Letni* Corporation. He set up a telephone conference with you today at three. You were free so I put it in the book."

Jason walked slowly to his inner office. "Oh, thanks. He doesn't call all that often. Any idea what he wants?"

"No. He didn't say and I didn't ask. I might have but he wasn't very conversant and I had the impression this is strictly between you and he."

"O.K."

Jason went into the library-storage room and re-trieved a personnel file he had put together on *Letni* employees at the middle management level. Usually when Alexander called it had something to do with management decisions or a problem employee.

He couldn't help notice that Greta had arranged his shelves with the legal decisions in chronological order and the law books numerically and alphabetically. Loose papers were set in three distinct trays, the table was clear of dust and debris and the room had been swept. Jason noted that the copy machine had been moved closer to a corner providing more space around the oblong table in the middle, the chairs were neatly arranged around the table and the two lamps strategically arranged affording maximum lighting and the overall appearance of order.

"I see you straightened things out a bit. Thanks."

"Yes, I'd like to buy an automatic coffee maker and some accessories. Maybe a small cooler or refrigerator. And a divider. Then you could take depositions in an orderly way and the place wouldn't look like a kitchen."

"Great, I have a petty cash account you can use."

And so it went, a working relationship based on mutual trust. As time went on Greta took on more responsibility for decision-making as Jason's trust level became ever more comfortable.

The call from Alexander related to concerns of some senior management people that coded and secured information might be less secure than otherwise thought. In particular one or two managers suspected that someone in middle management was removing industry sensitive material and copying it. Industrial espionage. Jason suggested the appropriate security avenues available including retaining a private firm to investigate. This was out of his field and he was comfortable in making a few suggestions and dismissing the matter.

Several months passed without any further discussion and the matter seemed to be dropped.

The office was running smoothly. Greta asked for some time off to be with her family during the

Thanksgiving holiday and Jason left for a coastal resort.

One of his clients operated a bookstore in Newport, Oregon and he went down to offer some suggestions on leasing arrangements and to spend a few relaxing days in the area.

While there he took a drive to Heceta Head and later visited the aquarium in Newport. At Yaquina Bay Lighthouse he learned that a Nancy Drew Mystery segment had been filmed there, but that was long before his time in Oregon. On Thanksgiving he took in the spectacular view from Boiler Bay and had dined at Salishan Lodge close by. He thought of solitude as being cleansing but, nevertheless, could not help but wonder what Greta might be doing at this time. Occasionally he thought of her. By Monday, Jason was ready to return to his law practice.

Jason kept his private life very separate from the office. His personal papers, including a copy of his will, were kept at his condo and he was careful to keep track of his own Visa receipts and other business related paraphernalia. In this way he maintained an individuality and separateness uncommon with many men. In short, he was his own person. The price to be paid was irrelevant to the need.

As the weeks passed Greta came to understand and respect this. She was also an individual in her own right. She came to respect Jason's sense of humanity - the way he treated clients, rich and poor alike, the pro bono cases he took, the ready availability he offered to younger colleagues and his sense of fairness. She came to appreciate his overriding sense of the law and its fullest implications for justice, an avenue by which people could expect to have predictability, however imperfect.

Jason was five foot, ten, dressed neatly, and kept

his hair short and his shoes shined. In a manner of speaking he reminded her of Harrison Ford. Yet, beyond this visage she came to understand the embodiment of a solid, predictable and humane man.

Jason thought of Greta in somewhat similar ways. Perhaps feminine. Her voice was enticing.

His Asian experiences had brought a deep appreciation of Buddhism and reincarnation. In idle moments he liked to think of how someone might be reincarnated, an odd pastime, to be sure, but one that brought some understanding to Jason. In a sense, he was lending his intuition prominence. With Greta he thought of her as the reincarnate of a cat-graceful and aloof. And there was that fragrance about her! It conjured up an unmistakable sentience of romance. An élan he could not understand.

The intercom buzzed abruptly and Jason was jolted to the immediacy of his vitality.

"Mr. Dieter Zook is here to see you." Greta's voice was clear, crisp and precise. When she spoke he knew exactly what to expect.

"Please send him in."

A slender, somewhat obsequious man in a three-piece suit quietly and hesitatingly entered the room and made immediate eye contact with Jason.

" Hello Mr. Zook, I'm Jason Knox, please call me Jason." He was careful not to use his sobriquet "Skip." This man before him exuded an air of intensity and resoluteness.

"Please call me Dieter." He remained solemn and spoke with an unmistakable Germanic accent.

Dieter Zook was clean-shaven, tall and slender to the point of anorexia. His sallow complexion conveyed an unmistakable message of illness. Clearly myopic, he wore wire-rimmed spectacles. The manifested nervousness was not unusual for a new client but the sense of impending doom was.

Jason became aware of his discomfort and tried to smile. There was something immediately unsettling about this man and his attire and conduct seemed out of place in Portland. Jason experienced a penetrating sense of this mans social alienation. Even the scent of his aftershave produced a discordant and alien ambience. He took all of this in saying nothing but the silence became awkward.

"What can I do for you Mr. Zook...Dieter?"

Jason realized he was thinking and speaking formally. He could not mitigate his sense of discomfort.

"I work at the *Letni* Corporation and have been a supervisor there for thirteen years, in the micro processing section. Before that I worked in the containment area, as my background is both, in engineering and software applications. I heard about you at the Company and you're highly thought of. You have the reputation of being a man of sterling character."

"Well, thank you but..."

Before Jason could finish Dieter interjected, "I've asked about you in the community as well, and people say you are very kind and very loyal to your clients."

Jason was not comfortable with what might be becoming sycophancy. He did not like to be fawned over.

"Then you've been checking up on me?"

"Well, maybe you could call it that."

" What do you call it, Mr. Zook?"

"Prudence. I'm bringing my life to you."

Jason had no way of knowing just how accurate this statement would turn out to be.

"Well, how can I help you then?"

"Mr. Knox...I would appreciate help in preparing

my will. I only have one surviving family member, my sister. She lives in Germany. I own a home in Hillsboro, some Columbia Mutual Funds, a few Tri-Met bonds and Treasury notes. There is also the possibility of joint ownership of property in Germany.

Dieter explained how he and his one year older sister were children during World War II. They had lived in Eastern Germany and were separated shortly after cessation of hostilities. Their parents had been killed, by the Russians during the invasion and subsequent occupation. Elisabett, his sister, remained in Schlieben but Dieter had escaped with his uncle who settled in Dortmund. The Wall prevented any direct communication. Dieter went on to University graduating with a degree in engineering. He had studied English intensely expecting to immigrate to the United States, as his uncle had died of complications of diabetes during the time Dieter was a university student. The *Letni* Corporation recruited him and he had settled in Portland, believing at first that he would be in Portland, Maine and close to New York, the city of his dreams.

Nevertheless he made the adjustment to America without undo difficulty and maintained contact with his homeland by membership in the German Society and various cultural activities, such as, helping to organize the October Fest at Mt. Angel every year. He maintained his staunch Roman Catholicism, worked hard and never married.

When the German reconciliation began and the DDR dissipated, Dieter relocated Elisabett and there followed an emotional reunion. He began to reestablish his property ownership rights visiting Germany whenever necessary to search out and document assets. From information given him in the past by his uncle and what he could learn by independent research, he believed these assets to be substantial. All East German property had been confiscated by the Communists after the takeover of the Russian Occupation.

The process of land reclamation was slow and Dieter repeatedly petitioned the German Government working his way through the bureaucracy-a tedious and unrewarding experience. The German Government, burdened by the new economic responsibilities of its Eastern inhabitants, was slow and cautious in responding. There was now a paper wall in place of a concrete one.

"Perhaps, Mr. Knox, you could help. In due time of course?"

By this time, Jason had become intrigued with the story of Dieter's plight. After all, in his own way, Felix Frankfurter had championed the "I Wobbly Wobblies" - the IWW, when others of lesser renown turned their backs on these disenfranchised people.

To Dieter, he responded that he would do what he could but that this would likely involve the expertise of an attorney skilled in International Law, especially if Dieter was also claiming property rights, as soon after his arrival in the United States, he had become an American citizen.

Silent for a moment, Dieter responded: " We can put this in abeyance for now but I do trust you, Mr. Knox, and hope you will be involved in some way.

Knowing Dieter would need money to breach the paper wall, more money than he could possibly earn, Jason nodded. He did not want to commit himself,

Dieter went on: "I am not in the best of health. I suffer from diabetes and take insulin-quite a bit of insulin. Doctor Nikoob at St. Vincent's hospital takes very good care of me. I am a difficult case, a special case. Nikoob is Board Certified in three different specialties, imagine that. He takes only the difficult cases.

This was the first display of emotion Jason had seen from this man. This man who was rapidly becoming his client. This man who, unbeknownst to him, would change his life forever.

Jason responded: "Well, Diabetes is a very treatable illness, Dieter."

"Yes, but my condition is complicated. Years ago I developed an infection. The doctors called it something like ascending cholangitis. It destroyed part of my pancreas, the gland that regulates sugar in the body. This makes my illness more difficult to treat and causes complications to appear sooner."

"I see," said Jason. "I'll help you however I can." He was sincere and took pleasure in being the good guy. A champion of this man who suffered during the war, lost his parents, became separated from his sister, had to establish himself in a new country and now suffered from an incurable disease that could produce major complications.

Frankfurter and Brandeis were coming to the fore again. It was Lincoln defending the common man - the boy accused of murder and the farmer who was losing his acreage. Clients like this would help conciliate his conscience. He would be more than the champion of a large corporation. After all, Lincoln had also been a railroad attorney, defending the rights of the wealthy. Jason, like Lincoln, wanted to do and did both. His elderly clients suffered from disabilities of various kinds and he championed their rights with insurance companies. He rarely sent such clients bills, donating hours of time to their needs. He was also known for his racial tolerance and not a few of his clients were Hispanic, Asian, Native or African American.

Jason outlined his polices, fees and anticipated expenses. He agreed to prepare Dieter's will.

Dieter left as quietly as he had come.

The ensuing few days were busy ones for Jason and fortunately Greta had reorganized the office in an efficient manner, greatly facilitating the rapidly increasing number of cases that were coming in.

Within four days Dieter called the office to set up another appointment to review his assets. He was somewhat touchy with Greta on the phone, insisting on a late afternoon or early morning time and sounding very conspiratorial.

In the meantime, Jason had settled three very difficult cases, one of which dealt with sexual harassment in the workplace. The other two dealt with wrongful job termination.

He had been the defense attorney on all three, representing the employer, and surmised that a jury would likely give away more money to the plaintiffs than he could settle the cases for. They were not substantial or necessarily valid claims, but the juries in Multnomah County had been showing an increasing tendency to give away money - especially if that money came from corporate employers or insurance companies. The juries knew that the companies were backed by insurance and had developed an increasing antagonism to these companies without realizing that the money was really coming out of their own or their children's pockets.

With some plaintiffs it was their moment in the limelight. With petty crybaby complaints, for the first time in their lives they could feel important. The lawyers paid attention to them and their potential largesse, the legal assistants paid attention and even the doctors who examined and testified for them seemed to pay attention. For a time these ordinary people became the protagonists - the central actors - on a stage set by promise of lucrative financial rewards. The lawyers made money, the doctors made money and, more often than not, the plaintiffs made money. The chance of the latter was greater if juries were involved and the plaintiff's attorneys did not hesitate to 'play the jury card'.

The insurance companies paid and the cost was passed on to the taxpayers in various forms - to the very people who sat on the juries and gave the money away.

In the workers compensation system, with which some of Jason's clients were involved, the system was more balanced, perhaps even egalitarian. This system utilized seasoned Administrative Law Judges in the decision-making role and they could judge the credibility of witnesses based on continuous experience and provide judgments based on points of law. If either party is dissatisfied, there is an opportunity to appeal a decision to the Worker's Compensation Board in Salem for further consideration.

After putting the paperwork for these cases in order, Greta mentioned to Jason that the office had received a number of invitations to holiday office parties hosted by some of the larger law firms in town. She thought it was a good idea if he attended some, as they were well attended by consultants of various kinds and meeting them socially made it easier to deal with them by phone when their services were requested for evaluation. She had learned from her former husbands practice that putting a face to a name greatly increased the chances of co-operation.

One such party hosted by the Bosco firm was especially pertinent to the work Jason was doing and Greta emphasized that there were twenty-seven attorneys in this firm with plenty of contacts and a friendly attitude toward Jason. The networking potential was substantial.

Jason was happy to be busy but also content when he had leisure time to read and wasn't too concerned about an enormous income. After all, he had no one to support but himself and, although his lifestyle was very comfortable, he was not extravagant. He liked to spend some of his time reading the legal decisions Lincoln had been involved in; especially since many of the Lincoln documents had been classified secret until relatively recent times. He was noncommittal to Greta's recommendations and suggested that she attend representing his office, adding almost as an afterthought that she should have a good time.

Dieter's second appointment with Jason was remarkably similar to the first. His suit was different and he carried what appeared to be a German language magazine but his behavior had not changed. This is a man, thought Jason, who went through life without emphasis - lackluster was the word.

"Here is a summary of my assets Mr. Knox. There are more specifics in my notebooks but this is the main body of material. These copies are for you."

The sheets revealed typed figures and organized lists of assets by name and number. Very German, thought Jason.

"Fine," he responded and they went on to discuss Dieter's last will and desires including specific requests to be carried out at the time of his death.

Dieter insisted on reviewing his life philosophy - his Weltanschauung, as he called it, and Jason listened with a combination of boredom and discomfort.

There was something about this man that did not

excite Jason - something that was missing.

The particulars ended. Dieter gathered up his remaining papers, placed them carefully in a worn imitation leather case and uttered, almost imperceptibly in an uneven voice, "Thank you very much Mr. Knox."

Jason nodded.

He was feeling tired by this time.

Almost as an afterthought, Dieter broke the silence: "Well, there is one more thing I hoped you could help me with."

Jason's edginess increased. When clients added the 'one more thing' scenario it usually meant a complication of some kind.

A psychoanalyst friend had told him that patients sometimes drop a bombshell at the end of the hour and then leave. Jason found this with his clients as well and they either wanted more time with him, wanted to evade an issue or simply to press a matter by surprise.

Jason, to his own surprise, responded abruptly: "What is it?"

"Well, I know you will keep my will in a safe place, and you know, Mr. Knox, I live alone and I am not well. I mean there aren't many people I can trust. Well, you know...I wondered if you would be able to keep some of my diaries and personal papers. I mean for safekeeping. I'm willing to pay any extra fees for this service and there won't be many."

Jason was getting tired of Dieter's obsequiousness and responded: "Does this have to do with the property in Germany?"

"Well, no...at least not directly and I really would appreciate the help. I have no one Mr. Knox."

The ambiguity bothered Jason but the matter, after all, didn't seem like a monumental request and it did appear reasonable to help an ailing man.

"That's fine-I can do that for you."

"Oh thank you Mr. Knox. I will be forever grateful for your help.

Somewhat taken back by the import of these words Jason blurted out: "Oh, it's not a big deal", regretting the phrase almost before he said it.

Clearly this was a big deal to Dieter.

Leaving the office Dieter cast a furtive glance at Greta

She saw it and sensed that he was studying her. She later told Jason that Dieter was an odd duck - he seemed to have a hidden agenda.

She felt he was creepy, like some of the men she had seen in New York subways. She sensed something sinister in his manner. Her husband had behaved a little like this near the end of their marriage only it was covered up somewhat by his assertiveness.

Jason outwardly rejected the idea of something sinister or hidden about Dieter. "No, not likely," he replied, "He's just an old bachelor."

During the next few weeks Dieter visited the office unannounced and at varying times. He would wait for Jason to finish with a client and then hand him a double reinforced, heavily sealed and taped, manila envelope approximately 12" by 9" and then leave. He always insisted on giving this directly to Jason and barely commented to Greta. Jason kept the parcels locked in his desk and transferred them out on a weekly basis, as was his custom in dealing with clients personal papers.

Christmas was ten days away.

Jason had no plans.

Greta was spending five days with her parents in Central Oregon. She had told Jason she was going to ski at Mt. Bachelor but he didn't know if she was seeing someone.

Almost as an afterthought she mentioned stopping off at the Bosco party on her way home.

After her departure, Jason remained in the office working on a brief.

One of his clients had been seriously hurt and although the insurance company accepted responsibility for payment of medical bills associated with physical damages they contested the diagnosis of Post Traumatic Stress Disorder and did not want to pay the patients psychiatrist. He would need an independent   medical-psychiatric examination and would need to hire another psychiatrist to examine his client to render an opinion on the psychiatric damages. Then possibly the battle of the experts would begin.

After an hour he realized he had done about all he could in the office. Later he would have to research some points of law at the Lewis and Clark Law library. Ever the scholar, there were times when he became a fixture there.

He remembered the party and having no plans for dinner he decided to stop by the Bosco firm. Although somewhat overcast the view of the Willamette and the Christmas boat lights would be nice to see from the fifteenth floor of the Ben Franklin building.

Jason walked into a party that had started hours before.

The office rooms were packed with people most of whom he barely recognized. They stood around central tables laden with food or by the makeshift bars set up at strategic places.

He made his way to one of these; a large table covered with a white tablecloth and lined with rows of

31

upside-down glasses, raised his voice above the background chatter, and ordered a double dry martini. Sipping the drink he took in a collage of colors and a maze of smiling, talking faces. Although he sensed a blurring of sensual experience it was therapeutic to be around so many animated people-whole in body and spirit and comfortable with one another and the setting.

Larry Bosco, the senior law partner, greeted Jason and ushered him toward one of several tables laden with smoked salmon trays and a large variety of hors d' vors - what Northwesterners called finger foods.

Jason feasted his eyes on this cornucopia, balanced his drink and plate in one hand, helped himself to the salmon and turned to find a place to sit and someone to talk to.

At that moment he spotted Greta through a doorway entrance of another room. She had apparently gone home and changed into a red dress. A string of blue octagonal sapphire stones rested on the light blue silk scarf that adorned her slender neck. Hair flowing freely about her shoulders and surrounded by men Greta was more animated than usual and Jason could not help but absorb her aura of femininity-the woman in her.

She gracefully, almost invisibly, transferred her champagne glass to her left hand, waved and smiled at Jason. At this moment her whole body smiled-she was radiant. Perhaps the gin was having an effect.

Jason felt unsteady and flushed. He waved back and jerked as he lurched forward toward Greta, but his ambivalence became inaction and his gait was suspended in mid-stride. He suddenly became aware that he longed for her.

Greta became a phantom in the distance and Jason left the party as alone as he had come. As alone as ever.

At home Jason thought of Sophie - a relationship that would never be. Would this be his fate in all relationships? He had a nagging sense that he might never allow himself to let go and to love. To completely abandon his defensive shell and allow himself the vulnerability necessary to love another human being.

Drifting off to sleep in that half awake, half asleep state he visualized an image of the Berlin Wall. Within minutes he was far away.

O, I have passed a miserable night.
So full of ugly sights, of ghastly dreams.

Shakespeare
Richard III I,4

"She wished
That heaven had made her such a man."

Shakespeare
Othello I,3

THREE

JASON

The postmark on the letter was distinctly German and the return address read:

Frau Elisabett Hansberger
21 Friedreich Strasse
Schlieben, Deutschland

The writing on the envelope reminded Jason of the villagers in East Czechoslovakia who had little occasion to write letters and rarely received one. Opening the letter slowly and deliberately he read:

"Herr Professor Knox,

My name is Heinrich Schmidt and I am writing on behalf of my dear friend Frau Elisabett Hansberger, who has little knowledge of English. Perhaps you will recognize her by her former name Elisabett Zook. Her brother, Herr Dieter Zook is one of your charges. He has great trust in you."

The letter went on to explain that Frau Hansberger was worried about her brother, as his behavior in recent months had changed dramatically. His telephone calls were intense and disjointed. The letter told Jason that Dieter was obsessed with the land reclamation issue since the wall had come down and she was concerned that his health would suffer. She also wanted to know if Dieter were in some kind of trouble and implored Jason to help and   protect her brother. She wanted him to convince Dieter that getting the land back at this stage of her life was of little importance. She thought her brother might be in some kind of danger. She explained that she was alarmed with the frantic quality of Dieter's last telephone call and that she would somehow pay for any additional work Jason might encounter in fulfilling her wishes. The letter was signed in German script: *"With great respect, Frau Elisabett Hansberger."*

Well...this added something to the mystery surrounding Dieter but, then again, it could all be explained by a brothers concern for a sister who, like him, had been a victim of the political consequences of the cold war. Still...what kind of danger could Dieter be in, and what were Jason's responsibilities as his attorney? Did Greta understand something about Dieter that he didn't?

He felt obligated to discuss this letter with Dieter but part of him wanted to put any disclosure on hold. I'll see what develops, he thought.

Greta approached him later in the day. Setting down a cup of black coffee on Jason's desk she uncharacteristically asked a question: "I saw the postmark on the envelope. Do you have a client in Germany, or was that a personal letter?"

The comment intruded into the silence of Jason's thoughts, yet he was soothed by her voice. Outside her presence he had bonded with her voice, as if he had physically taken the sound in. A sound resonating her thoughts, becoming his thoughts. She seemed almost too good to be true. The content of her words transcended their literal meaning and the sound announced her presence within his psyche. There, in that very moment, existed for Jason a commingling of life forces-of an intimate experience. In a few short months the rhythms of his body had become attuned to her touch, smell, body heat, muscle tension and visage. Mystically he could conjure her up and see, hear and feel her presence, a circumstance he only gradually became aware of. It was beyond his conscious volition.

As if returning from an infinite distance he responded: "Oh, just business"-sipping the coffee "thanks."

Greta knew enough to back off and quietly left the room.

Jason's curiosity about Greta increased over time.

Once when she was off on an errand he noticed a book she had been reading: *The Architecture of Creativity-Profiles Behind the Mask.*" She had made notes in Chapter 2 about Wyeth's use of egg tempera and he recalled her earlier comment.

That night his dreams were filled with huge eggs tumbling down a hillside and brushing by him like huge rubber balls. It was not altogether unpleasant.

The following morning he seized an impulse to walk over to the Art Museum library. A slender, flirtatious young assistant helped him select three books on the artist Andrew Wyeth. He was welcome to read them at the library as only art students and professors had check out privileges.

Two hours later he left to meet an attorney he sometimes worked with as co-counsel. She and her husband had a sailboat and during summer months Jason sailed with them on the Columbia River. She was someone he could confide in about most anything. They spent the afternoon discussing a case.

Jason returned home, poured a drink and sat daydreaming.

His thoughts referenced the Wyeth material he had read and the Pennsylvania landscape, as well as, familiar sounding, German family names like Kuehner, Miller and Zitselsberger. In his mind the library reading fused with the letter from Elisabett and stirred up memories from another life-a different time.

During the cold war the CIA placed operatives in strategic places throughout the world, a process that has continued to the present day. The American supplied physician to the Burmese premier was a covert agent, as was the attendant to the French Ambassador in London who reported to the "control" agent at the American Embassy. There were also people who functioned as NOC's-non-official cover-including businessmen, students and professors not technically employed by the United States Government.

Jason's past life had encompassed all of this and more.

CIA psychiatrists picked his dossier out of hundreds, as he fit the "profile", to serve as a go-between with a potential head of State and the U.S. government. This brought Jason to Czechoslovakia to await the release of an imprisoned political organizer whose potential for leadership within the Czech government was high. He came to the international community somewhat indirectly serving initially with the Army's Defense Intelligence Agency and later with the U.S. Air Force. He was known as a "reliable" and became a covert agent go-between reporting to the CIA.

During this time he met Sophie, an idealisticly driven woman, who risked her life to help him and with whom he initiated an affair that began as a matter of convenience and ended up as a deep passion. In fact, the deepest love of his life.

Under the circumstances the fruition of this love would never materialize on a lasting basis.

Sophie was Czech down to the bone and the CIA's recognition of Jason's deepening attachment and emotional dilemma led to his transfer.

The "operation" could not be compromised. Ambivalence regarding a Stateside assignment is one thing but with an agent in the field it is career deafening.

Jason was reassigned to the CIA-Navy project dealing with underwater "signatures" of Soviet submarines, some of which still involved the Dolphin program. Dolphins had been taught to differentiate the "signatures" of Soviet submarines and were part of the underwater weapons delivery system. During this time some of the Dolphins seemed to commit "suicide" or at least engaged in self-destructive behavior.

Jason wanted out of this and his transfer to Langley was finally accepted. There he worked on the defector-deception studies.

The initial work had been done, by a well-known psychoanalyst, during the 1960's and it was this work that led Jason to Portland.

Sitting alone in his condo his memories were bittersweet. He sought solace in sleep, but his was a restless night.

He faced the finely polished wooden boxes and puzzled at the task before him. These objects were familiar nocturnal visitors. Something had to be done, but what? This dream was hauntingly evocative of something. Frustration led to anxiety, which led to panic. Demons inside

His feelings broke through the barrier and he awakened abruptly and screamed in silence.

Years before this dream had announced its importance. It had been deciphered. No longer a secret and now a permanent fixture. A psychic shibboleth meant to master and to undo the original traumas. The flight back from Cam Ran Bay would have been routine perhaps even uneventful had it not been for the "cargo" on board.

Jason sat against the fuselage of the 141 Starlifter strapped in a parachute rack and could only wonder in puzzlement at the meaning of it all. There was no meaning. The wooden caskets were piled in neat stacks-three rows across and endlessly deep. Intermittently he caught glimpses of the flight crew through the open cockpit door silhouetted against a beautifully star studded sky. He was the only living passenger and above the drone of the engines he could make out the moans and groans and creaking coming from the crated coffins. With altitude, changes in pressure created strange sounds. Air rushed thru the organs of bodies that had been living only days perhaps hours before. Young men, some of whom he had known, going home. Moving body limbs made sounds indistinguishable from the creaking of the polished containers, containers with the sacrificial remains of an ancient holy right-war.

But which memory was reality?

Which the dream?

He could no longer tell.

It was 2 AM. Perspiration beaded on his face and

forehead and his neck was wet with sweat.

He awoke thinking of Greta and wanting to see her he reached for the phone, dialed and waited-the ringing seemed interminable. Then a voice-*the* voice.

"Hello...hello?"

"Hi Greta."

"Jason?...Hello?"

"Yes."

"It must be the middle of the night. What's wrong?"

"Oh, I just thought of something I wanted to talk over with you. Can I come over?"

"Can't it wait till morning?"

"Oh. I guess so..."

Greta, now more fully awake, could hear the hesitancy and emotional intensity of Jason's comments. She instinctively knew something was wrong. She sensed Jason's urgency and felt he needed her.

"No, it's o.k. Come on over. Please come. I'll make some tea."

The streets were empty and the drive from Jason's condo at the marina to Greta's place in the West Hills was brief.

She heard his car pull up, opened the door before he rang the bell and motioned him into the living room.

"Jason, you look like hell. What's happened?"

"Oh, just a bad dream I wanted to talk to somebody."

Hearing this Greta was irritated- a flash of anger. "Somebody? Somebody!! You come here in the middle of the night to talk to *somebody* about a bad dream?"

Jason had no words. He began to cry.

She sensed his vulnerability and walked toward him.

Greta wrapped her arms around him and pulled his face to hers.

Hesitating momentarily he kissed her - gently at first.

Her tongue touched his and suddenly she thrust it into his mouth furiously kissing and sucking his lips and face. Her eyes rolled back, his closed. He pulled his sweater off and they began rolling on the thinly matted carpet as she helped him undo his belt and pushed his pants off. Greta's nightgown was open and Jason cupped her breasts and began ever so gently rubbing her nipples and they quickly became hard and erect. He was surprised at the depth of her passion as she pulled him ever closer wrapping her legs around his hips. She thrust her body backwards arching her hips as she reached and put him inside her.

The writhing went on for an eternity and a millisecond as they twisted and rolled furiously, ensconced in sexual ecstasy. They clinged. The liquidness of her drew him ever closer. The eternity passed and Jason rolled on to his side while Greta continued to breathe heavily. He was motionless. Soon her breathing shallowed and they both were silent.

She spoke first. " Well, that was a surprise."

"Yes," Jason responded, "it was."

They spent the night in close embrace. In the morning, after coffee, they drove to work in silence. Two lovers in a world without words.

He was wont to speak plain and to the purpose, like an honest man and a soldier; and now his words are a very fantastical banquet.

Shakespeare
Much Ado About Nothing II,3

FOUR

PAUL

Jason was deep in thought when the intercom buzz startled him. Greta's voice was crisp and direct: "Mr. Paul Howieson here to see you Mr. Knox. He doesn't have an appointment but asked if he could have just a few minutes of your time. He said it's an urgent personal matter about someone named Sophie."

Jason was startled again. He paused: "Send him in. And Greta, ah, ah...hold my calls."

The door opened and closed quietly. A tall, muscular clean-shaven man dressed in a dark blue business suit with gray pin stripes stood before Jason's desk.

"Hello Mr. Knox." Simultaneously brandishing credentials, he spoke in a strong voice with the command presence Jason knew well: "I'm Special Agent Paul Howieson, FBI"

Jason's could feel his heart miss a beat. He swalled. "Err...hello. People call me Skip." Regaining his composure he quipped: "I haven't robbed any banks lately. What does the FBI want with me? Is this a personal matter?" Jason motioned Paul to a chair. He thought of the comment about Sophie.

Paul responded: " I used Sophie's name to get your attention. We can talk about her later if you like. I read your dossier Mr. Knox. I know a great deal about you. I'll get right to the point 'Skip'. This is not personal, it's about Dieter Zook, AKA Dieter Zucher, AKA Dieter Zimmermann."

Jason was caught off guard and stunned at the disclosure. He knew enough about intelligence work to discern that the FBI would not be visiting him without a good reason. He hesitated in disclosing that Dieter was his client but thought that they must know he was somehow connected with him. Why else would a special agent be visiting him? He was curious about the AKA's. Paul caught him off guard. As one of the FBI's finest counterintelligence officers he was a pro at what he did. Even the CIA spoke highly of Paul, high praise coming from a sometimes rival agency.

"Well...ah...I can't say much about a client you know. Lawyer-client privilege." His voice trailed off.

"A dead client" countered Paul.

Once again Jason was thrown off balance. This was a morning of surprises. "What do you mean? Dieter dead? What happened?"

"Officially, he died of complications of diabetes. Unofficially... Well...lets discuss that later."

Jason immediately grasped the importance of this comment. He suspected Dieter had been murdered. Why else would the FBI be here?

Death was no stranger to Jason, but he wasn't sure how much he would or could share with the FBI or anyone for that matter. In death an attorney represents the decedent's estate and he knew that the courts had not fully ruled on issues of confidentiality in postmortem representation. "What do you want with me?"

"You're a special guy Skip-the Bureau knows a

little about you."

"Oh, how so?"

Paul began a recitation almost as if he was reading from the dossier: " Jason Knox, AKA Lawrence Wright, code name Blue Fox, former United States Air Force Intelligence, Viet Nam service, Bronze Star, covert intelligence agent 1970, secret intelligence commendation signed by the President..."

"O.K., O.K., that's enough."

"Quite a record for a graves registration officer. A good cover. We know you consulted a CIA psychiatrist after this duty."

Jason was getting hot and responded abruptly: "Get to the point."

Paul was very smooth. Nonplussed he opened a leather briefcase and produced some photos. "These are surveillance photos. Do you recognize anything here?"

Jason responded sarcastically: "A telephone booth?"

"The person Mr. Knox, the person."

The tension was building between them.

"Superman?" replied Jason.

Howieson became more formal and officious: "O.K. Mr. Knox that's your former client, known to you as Dieter Zook."

"So what, he makes telephone calls. So do I."

"We were tracing his calls. We've learned some interesting things about Dieter Zook. We also had a dossier about him here at the Portland office but it was buried deeper than King Tut."

Jason's curiosity was aroused. "How so?"

One of your attorney colleagues served in the U.S. Army in Germany sometime after the war. The so-called repatriated Germans were given jobs at American military installations and your colleague became familiar with them and noted, with substantial aversion, their continuing Nazi sympathies. Years later he discovered, quite by accident, that one of the more vehement and obnoxious of them had settled in Portland. Well, you can guess it. Dieter Zook never expected to meet the likes of Victor Carlson, attorney at law.

Jason *could* guess the rest. He knew Carlson was a champion of the underdog and had a passion for fairness that crossed racial and socioeconomic boundaries. In short, a man of principle who could not be bought, whatever the stakes.

"The rest is history. One of our agents started a zero file and the information was stored away. In a similar circumstance Klaus Fuchs, the atomic spy, was apprehended when one of our agents in Germany found his name on a list of Communist Party members and sympathizers that had been compiled by Nazi Intelligence agents. His "cut out" in the U.S. was Harry Gold, a technician who worked at Philadelphia General Hospital. Two pieces of a Jello box and the two traitors made history. Ancient history now."

In providing this background, Paul was cleverly appealing to Jason's sense of history, elevating the current concerns with a major espionage case. He meant to intensify the drama and peak Jason's interest.

"I know history but what's this have to do with Dieter or with me for that matter?"

"Dieter Zook was being blackmailed by Israeli intelligence. The Mossad. They agreed to keep his Nazi affiliation buried in return for classified information. I can tell you that some of this had to do with the technical aspects of the SURTASS, the surveillance towed array system on our nuclear submarines and some on the multiple warhead reentry data for missiles. The Polaris system on our subs was of major interest. Much of this intelligence material is outdated but the improvements continue and are significant."

Having served on the *USS Pogy,* a nuclear attack submarine, Jason understood the significance of what Paul was telling him. But he wondered where all of this fit in with Dieter and now with himself. He asked the obvious. "Aren't the Israeli's our allies?" This was a rhetorical question, as he knew the answer. He remembered the attack on *The Liberty.*

"Well, in a way," Paul responded. "But they also spy on us and know how to procure equipment...there's a kind of unofficial, unrecognized kind of espionage. We in the Bureau worry about it but politics supercede our interest and the national interest. I don't have to tell you that."

Paul's comments struck a cord.

"But if that was the case Zook was antithetical to everything the Israel State stands for."

"Necessity is the mother of invention my dear Mr. Knox. Zook's sins were minor compared to Eichman. Zook passed orders on and facilitated the rounding up of Jews in Hungary and Italy but, and it's a big but, he didn't issue any direct orders or make any decisions himself. The Catholic Church under Pope Pius stood by as well when Jews were rounded up in Italy and Hungary and shipped to the camps. No one has a monopoly on indifference or for that matter cruelty. The Israelis are acutely aware of history; they live history and have for thousands of years. Using Zook for the greater good justifies the oversight of his character and behavior. You know as well as I do - espionage is a tough game. By the way Pius may never be declared a Saint because of his inaction in the face of human atrocities. Sorry, I'm getting away from the issues here. Don't mean to preach." Once again, Paul was intensifying the sense of drama.

Jason responded quietly and somberly: "Not at all, this helps me put things in perspective. I appreciate your candidness." Jason found himself sympathetic to Paul's perspective.

"Jason, it is even more complicated than this but I don't want to go into it now...Dieter was playing the angles. He had a German passport in his possession when he died. There were also copies of *Der Stern* with coded ads corresponding to ads in *The Jerusalem Times*. I wish we could take credit for this but German G-7 people tipped off our agents. This led to the surveillance."

Jason listened intently, his uneasiness increasing with each word Paul spoke. "O.K., O.K. but what do you want with me. Please get to the point."

Jason's irritation increased but it was not because of Paul's behavior. Jason thought in patterns and, in his mind, a pattern was emerging . His expression became dour. He also understood the FBI technique of giving a little information to get more, yet his curiosity was aroused. Mostly the FBI gave nothing in terms of meaningful data but Jason was hearing something that was clearly confidential. He was aware of the FBI's reputation for arrogance and began to sense condescension. A mixture of emotions flooded his consciousness. Paul seemed much more sensitive than most agents. The agents from the Hoover days were either retiring or dying off and the "I'm holier than thou" attitude was being replaced with a more cooperative business demeanor, especially with the recruitment of Hispanic and Blacks and even more so with their advancement to supervisory positions . Attitudes filtered down from the top. Jason also knew of the Bureau's penchant for grandstanding. When something sensational happened, like a murder or celebrity kidnap, the local police did most of the work and the Feds would come in, take the credit and grab the headlines. Jason had been around long enough in government as well as legal circles to understand this. He was nobody's fool and not about to be used for someone's purpose let alone their glory. He sensed what was coming.

Paul broke the silence: "We'd like your help Jason."

"How is that?"

"I can't go into all the details until we have a commitment from you. I can say that we need the information you have and we also want someone to work with us. You are on the outside of this operation. An innocent bystander and that's good."

Jason did not care for the word 'commitment'. He also noticed Paul's use of the word 'until' instead of 'unless'. It was as if Jason was given no choice. Someone had already decided he would cooperate. He quickly regretted his lawyer-like response: "Well, I need to know more about this."

Paul was silent.

"I'll, I guess I'll think about it. This is all new to me. I'm a practicing attorney with responsibilities to my clients and the community.

Paul responded without hesitation: " You are in this already Jason. You are up to your ears."

The familiar FBI arrogance.

A long silence followed, broken by Paul:

"We have reason to believe that your life is in danger."

"Danger? Why danger? Me? I'm not one of your spooks."

If his comments were meant as an insult Paul showed no reaction. "Well...you have been involved with a client whom we suspect of deep cover espionage and more. The people who are after him know that you have information they want. They believe you and Dieter were partners and they will stop at nothing to get what they want."

"You say *more* than espionage. What's the 'more' part of this?"

"I can't tell you anything else at this time." Paul's words were sharp and concise. "We need a commitment."

Jason thought of marriage when he heard that word 'commitment'. He didn't like the idea of being bound. He repeated the word: 'commitment'.

"Well, look at it any way you like. The point is we need your help. This is not about money and it's not about you or me. I don't want to give you a patriotic spiel that sounds trite and stupid. You've been around the corner a few times."

Jason appreciated being spared a song and dance. He responded reasonably: "Give me some time to think about this. It's all so... so...new."

"Fine, but don't take too long. This isn't the midnight train to Georgia. Timing is of the essence and we don't want to see anyone else killed."

With these remarks, Paul stood up, extended his hand to Jason, expressed a collegial smile and left the office. Greta watched him leave:

"Bye now."

Paul turned briefly and nodded.

How beauteous mankind is! O brave new world,
That hath such people in 't!

Shakespeare
The Tempest, V,1

FIVE

ALEXANDER

Jason was running late for his luncheon date with Greta.

She was nervously looking at her watch when he arrived at Papa Haydens, a trendy restaurant in the Northwest section of Portland. She was seated by the window, gazing. Jason took in her visage complete with designer jeans and black sweater-a slender refined gold necklace fit snugly around her neck. Understated as usual. Jason noticed that she was wearing a colorful inlaid bracelet on her right wrist and her Tiffany watch on the left, barely protruding from the edge of her sweater.

"Hi, sorry I'm late."

Greta did not respond and seemed out of sorts. Her expression was sour.

"Nice bracelet."

"I collect them. This is Zuni-direct from the reservation."

Her voice was strained and he felt awkward.

"Ordered yet?" he asked, already knowing the answer.

"No. I was waiting for you."

On the drive over Jason found himself wondering about her seeming enthusiasm for a relatively mundane job, her curiosity about his letter from Germany expressed so nonchalantly. For that matter how had she arrived so early and gained entrance to his office on her first day of work? And why before him? She also seemed to have taken a singular aversion to Dieter Zook, or at least it seemed that way. Jason speculated that Dieter would do nearly anything to help his sister buy back the land. Was this just his imagination? Was her arrival and his representation of Zook a coincidence? The secret agent and the lawyer in him had fused and raised these questions. By the time he pulled up in front of the restaurant he had dismissed these thoughts and now he found himself face to face with a beautiful woman who was clearly annoyed. The tension between them was slowly building and he could not bring himself to believe it was because he was 20 minutes late.

"I suggest the club sandwich, Jason. You like turkey and the sandwiches are freshly made here."

She had, over time, learned a lot about his likes and dislikes especially where food was concerned. Greta learned early on that he had a strong dislike for candy and desserts and a predilection for Asian food, especially Korean. She had learned little about his family, however, and his biographical background was a mystery that had barely been sketched out in their time together. She had been much more open and emotionally telling about her relationship to her family and past relationships.

Jason ordered the turkey club and Greta picked at a shrimp salad.

"Are you O.K.? I mean you seem so quiet today. Upset because I was late?"

"No. I'm fine. Besides I had a chance to relax and study the menu while I was waiting and watching people on Northwest 23rd.

Jason was decidedly uncomfortable and lost for words. They both ate silently.

Jason had no way of knowing that some distance west of where he was sitting a young woman was going to work. This woman's life would become intertwined with his to such an extent that it would change his life forever. She would play a role in placing him as the protagonist in the most intense and dangerous adventure of his life. As with all such circumstances we are not in a position to be in control of our fate. For better or for worse we unwittingly become the objects of a giant chess game possibly but not necessarily controlled by a universal power.

Susan Lee turned off highway 26, followed Cornelius road south and made a right turn on to Evergreen Highway. A short distance down the road, off to the left, loomed the massive building complex of the Letni Corporation.

This was one of several groups of buildings, in Oregon and Washington, housing the most up to date technology in the world. The high technology centers of our age, and the technocrats who created it.

In front of the drive an unassuming blue sign was tastefully placed. In white letters it bore the name *Letni* with the "e" slightly displaced evocative of the artistic flair of the corporate designer.

Susan turned into the parking lot and parked next to the shuttle bus used for transporting employees to different buildings on the campus. Their motors were running.

Facing the main lobby she entered RA1 and faced the three security guards in blue uniforms, their finely polished gold badges sparkling. One guard, a large man in short selves had a massive tattoo of a ship that was immediately visible as he turned towards her. He nodded. She signed the register and he handed her an ID badge.

Susan had been working at *Letni* for more than two years and knew the routine pretty well. She had relocated from Vancouver B.C., and had lived in Seattle for a year before taking the job in Hillsboro, a suburb of Portland. Her co-workers liked her but knew little of her personal life other than that she had been born in Taiwan and had some college education. On breaks she spent most of her time with the Asian employees joining in the conversation with Chinese men, who reciprocated her interest. She was unattached and attractive and never at a loss for a lunch partner or company at break time. In fact, the Asian men held her in high regard.

The *Letni* Corporation had facilities in Beijing, China, as well as Israel. Although, for security reasons, sensitive high tech information was meticulously considered before being sent to overseas facilities, whose function was to produce common computer hardware.

Nevertheless, the French, Israeli's and Chinese would send their engineers on exchange programs to the Hillsboro facility, the original facility, to snoop around and learn what they could. The New China News Agency (N.C.N.A.) a cover for Chinese espionage operations had even sent reporters, ostensibly for a public relations story linking the Beijing operation with the Hillsboro facility. The FBI did not have advance information on this visit and it wasn't until the Chinese delegation left that the full recognition of their activities became known. This 'penetration' did not sit well with the supervisory agents in Washington, and the politicians turned a deaf ear to any concern. Chinese espionage in the United States had been an uphill battle for U.S. intelligence agencies, they had been hampered by political disinterest, monied interests and official indifference. The 'most favored nation' treaties, while possibly having an overall economic value, had cast an air of 'friendliness' and good will in the business and political communities in their relationship to Mainland China.

The facility security team was headed by an intelligent, long-term employee, Mack, who was 'politic' about the infra structure of the organization. With both industrial as well as political-national espionage experience he and his team had more than enough to keep them busy. They cultivated a close relationship to the Hillsboro police and the FBI. However, day in and day out the responsibility and grunt work remained with Mack and his team. They also had immediate access to any of the *Letni* facilities around the world. Simply by dialing 8 on any facility telephone they could access production in, for instance, the Philippines by providing the proper codes. They could also access computer data of individuals working on specific projects with security concerns.

Susan was reporting early for her shift. She had planned a brief vacation with some friends at the Central Oregon Sun River Resort and was working extra each day. The *Letni* Corporation was very flexible with their employees and this was one of the many benefits that made working there so attractive. She turned right, then left and walked down the long hallway in the direction of the lithograph division. The 'yellow rooms' were on her right. The employees inside were wearing white 'bunny suits' and moving deliberately and slowly. To an outsider this would seem like a science fiction movie. Off to the side, reactor operators studiously watched the robotic equipment as it silently placed the silicon wafers in the epi gas containers. These were adjacent to the wafer "boats" transferring consolidated wafers for processing. It was the quietness and almost stillness of it all that fascinated Susan, who, quiet by nature, could become a chameleon and blend into the fabric of the project.

She descended the wide staircase making sure to hold the railing on the way down. Failure to do so would result in a steep fine and, worse yet, a safety violation write-up being placed in her employee personnel file.

Susan avoided undo attention at all costs and already had a reputation as a trustworthy employee-a hardworking industrious Asian.

Once in the subterranean work area, she donned a pair of safety glasses and hard hat, placed a pair of ear plugs in her pocket and reported to the supervisor-her "lead" for the shift. There was little verbal exchange, as she knew her job well. The company thought of everything. Along the side wall every fifteen or twenty feet emergency showers with eye levage devices had been placed, allowing quick access in the event of a spill. The rule was twenty minutes of dousing followed by donning the emergency clothing that hung in plastic bags outside the showers.

Susan occasionally worked two floors above where the "brain trust" spent most of their time in isolated modules. Occasionally she used the "travel works" station, an enclosed area in different parts of the buildings complete with computer and other hardware thus allowing access to data from an individuals 'mainframe' in their own work area, wherever that might be. Mostly she worked in the lower level. But this was not the world of Greta and Jason.

They each had little to say. Jason thought he had better things to do than fathom the mind of a pouting woman and Greta seemed anxious to get back to the office. They parted amicably.

Jason set out to do some detective work of his own. The offices of the Carlson law firm clearly reflected the denizens' success, with an ornate exterior, inlaid gold trim around the entrance leading to a waiting room decorated with antique furniture.

The secretary who greeted Jason was of Greta's stature.

Carlson had been a police officer in Chicago during the '68 Democratic Convention and the riots. A huge photograph of the Chicago skyline adorned one wall of his inner office. He had presented his version of the historical events on a local radio station but now Jason was interested in another kind of history and he hoped to obtain all the information he sought after.

Carlson substantiated Paul's version of the events surrounding Dieter and his identity discovery, but he had little to add, although his dislike for the man was still clearly evident. Carlson almost snarled when mentioning his name and his sarcastic comments, a court-room trademark, were right on target. He had read about Dieter's death in the *Oregonian* and had no comment.

After leaving the Morrison Street law office, Jason placed a call to Roy Frank, the acting U.S. District Attorney for Oregon. He confirmed Paul Howieson's identity as an FBI agent in good standing and secured Frank's promise to forget he asked.

He did learn that Paul was highly regarded in the D.A.'s office as well as his peers. He was thorough and his cases stood up in court. The last one he had investigated involved the murder of an Anglo on the Warm Springs Reservation. Paul's work resulted in exonerating a Native American who had been accused of the crime and implicated a domestic partner of the deceased who was later charged and found guilty based on DNA evidence, as well as drug involvement.

Jason would be in good hands. Still...people, even FBI agents made mistakes. Jason had learned the hard way that no one was infallible.

After the call to Frank he drove to Dieter's apartment but couldn't gain entrance. He didn't really know what he was looking for anyway and decided to visit the Immigration and Naturalization Service.

After a substantial wait and a bucketful of politeness directed to a middle-aged secretary, the INS Records Division produced no results in a search for a Dieter Zook.

"Could the records have been expunged?" asked Jason.

"Why, who would want to do that?" responded the records clerk incredulously.

Jason decided to cease his questioning. Perhaps if he were a Federal Agent the responses would be different. But he wasn't and his leads were drying up. Besides he was getting tired. All of this fussing on top of a busy practice was beginning to wear thin. And even his relationship with Greta seemed strained.

He had one more visit to make.

Dr. Nikoob's office was quiet. Eerily so. The elderly nurse-receptionist ushered Jason in immediately upon his arrival. The doctor was waiting, sitting behind a large mahogany desk, an open file before him.

Prior to his arrival Jason had telephoned the doctor and explained that as Dieter's attorney he had full legal authority over his medical records. He had a few questions about the decedant's health.

"I went through this with the FBI", the doctor explained. "They had a court order for the records. I hope that was O.K.".

Jason thought the doctor seemed worried and

sought to put him at ease.

"No problem, doctor. I just wanted some clarification myself."

Dr. Nikoob went on the explain that Dieter's diabetes was under control, he had no infections, he was careful with his diet and he had monitored his blood sugars with the latest technology. In short there had been no reason for him to die.

The pathologist who did the autopsy was assigned to St. Vincent's hospital. He found no cause of death and could only speculate.

The FBI laboratory later requested and received laboratory samples of blood and urine along with some tissue slides that had been prepared. The results were not made available for Nikoob, although he had expressed an interest, hoping to learn something about helping his living patients. Dieter's death was a mystery.

Jason thanked the doctor and left, feeling more bewildered than ever.

The FBI was keeping their information to themselves.

Or had they even learned anything? One thing for sure, he was in the dark.

Driving back to his office he noticed a blue Mercedes following him. Was this the same car that had parked across the street from Dieter's apartment a few hours ago? Was he being followed? He dismissed the idea. An overactive imagination. Clearly he was taking things too seriously. He was spooking himself.

Once back in his condo, he began to prepare for a brief court appearance the following day and a one hour lecture presentation he was to give at the Personnel Law Update Program for Continuing Legal Education.

Jason had a restless night. In his dreams he was trying to read something important but couldn't make out the letters. The alphabet seemed strange and didn't fit together. He felt he was expected to climb a high wall that was very colorful at the top. It was one of those dreams where you knew something and how something was to be, but you hadn't experienced it yet. You worked to experience it and the more you worked the more tired you became. Jason woke up feeling exhausted. Psychiatrists call it non-restorative sleep. Jason called it yuck. He was clearly in it.

Jason was thankful that his day was relatively uneventful. The court hearing was over quickly and without complications. By the time he gave his portion of the lecture in the afternoon the audience was sleepy and had few questions. He was again thankful.

He phoned Greta to ask her to meet him at Jo Bar, a restaurant close by, for a drink and light dinner.

She was in a much better mood than when they last met and she looked almost radiant.

She filled him in on the calls for the day and brought along his appointment calendar.

Jason was tired and not interested in his schedule.

The wine they were drinking had gone to his head and he suggested they call it a day.

Greta asked if he would like to spend the night at her place.

Jason agreed and looked forward to an evening with Greta. He envisioned himself as needing tender loving care.

They weren't even through the doorway when Greta pulled Jason toward her and kissed him on his slightly open lips. As he turned toward her she reached her hand inside his belt, between his legs and began massaging his genitals.

Startled and aroused Jason immediately became erect.

He pulled her blouse off without undoing the buttons, quickly undid her bra and began kissing her nipples.

She undid her skirt and Jason slid his mouth down her torso, pulling her panties off, stopping to kiss and suck her naval. He moved his hands around to her buttocks and with head now between her legs began to swirl his tongue inside her. He absorbed her fragrance.

Now writhing in ecstasy Greta grabbed his member and thrust him inside her. She had longed for this moment. She had become acutely aware of her need for him.

Jason had also come to realize that Greta was the embodiment of all that he could love. An idealization of the ideal woman.

For an instant he thought of her at the Bosco party. The red dress adorned with blue sapphire stones and being gawked at by the men there.

There is a moment in everyone's life where time should stand still. This was that moment for both Jason and Greta. They were in complete harmonious resonance. They made passionate love on the thick carpet without a need for words.

As soon as he hit the bed and her soft mattress he was sound asleep, this time very deeply.

Jason found that he slept best when Greta was with him in the same room.

She woke up before him, prepared a light breakfast allowing him time to finish up paper work he had neglected for the past two days.

They drove separately to the office, Jason taking a detour to the courthouse to look up some documents pertaining to property that might have been owned by Dieter Zook. Again, no luck. Another dead end.

He drove back to the office almost overlooking

the police squad cars outside.

Resuming command, though anxious, Greta greeted him in the hallway to his office.

"Oh, Jason, someone has ransacked the office. It's a mess. I called the police as soon as I saw it and didn't go in. The detectives are dusting for prints now."

Jason tried to enter his office but was blocked by a burley police officer. He looked in and could only think of an old political expression that a defeated Presidential candidate once uttered-it was complete and devastating,

"Anyone you know that might be your enemy Mr. Knox," uttered the detective, in what sounded like a New York Bronx accent.

Jason looked at the mess in astonishment. At first the realization of a possible connection with Zook didn't dawn on him. He looked at Greta whose face evidenced a puzzled expression. The connection began to take hold as he responded: "No, not really. Lawyers do make enemies. I guess I have my share."

"Well if you can think of anyone in particular, who is looking for something, let us know. Maybe you could make a list of possible suspects. It don't look like nothin' valuable was taken. At least that's what your secretary said. Lawyers don't keep money or drugs in the office so I guess they're lookin' for something else." The detective's expression was bland.

As an afterthought he introduced himself. "I'm detective Alexander, Portland P.D. They call me Alexander. If you think of anything, call me." He handed Jason his card.

The remainder of the day was spent putting things back in place. It took hours since nothing was left unturned. The pillow cushions and a few other items were destroyed, but Greta was right, nothing valuable was taken.

Greta was shaken and Jason suggested she go

home and relax. He would come by later for a drink.

Jason tried to put a call through to Paul Howieson but couldn't reach him. He decided not to leave a message. He didn't know why he was calling him anyway. The damage had been done and he wasn't even sure this was connected to the Dieter Zook case. In his mind now it was "a case."

He drove home and found the front door of his condominium open. Another shock. Jason ran downstairs and phoned the police. He waited until they arrived before going inside.

The uniformed officer entered with gun drawn but Jason assumed that by this time the perpetrator or perpetrators were long gone. He surmised they were professionals. The place was a mess. Some of the wine bottles were broken and the wine shelf tossed across the floor. The officers had asked Jason to wait for the detectives to arrive and cautioned him not to touch anything.

About a half hour later detective Alexander arrived.

"Well...this is your bad day. Wow...what a mess."

Jason didn't need the commentary.

As Alexander went about dusting for prints and looking over some of the damaged objects Jason thought of him as a prototype police detective. To Jason he was a paradigm of the mess he was in. Alexander was a symbol of the mystery he sensed and the fear. Yes, he was beginning to be afraid. The person or persons who had entered his office and condo probably had not found what they were looking for. In fact Jason was beginning to acknowledge that they surely had not found what they wanted and wondered what was next. He felt lost. Neither Alexander nor Howieson could help him. He wanted out of this mess as quickly as possible and wondered what would be the best way to extricate himself. How could he convince his supposed enemies that he did not want to be a part of their intrigue and would surely give most anything to be left alone to practice law?

"Good night Mr. Knox. Watch yourself. If I were you I'd be careful."

Alexander left Jason standing in the middle of his condo amidst the shambles.

He did not respond.

The soul of this man is his clothes.

Shakespeare
Alls Well That Ends Well II,5

SIX

DAVID

In 1966 China launched its first nuclear weapon carried by a guided missile. China's Secret Service had begun stealing atomic secrets from the West beginning as early as 1946. This group early on compiled a register of all known Chinese scientists and students living in the United States, France, England and Germany. At least two hundred people on this list were leaders in their fields of higher mathematics and advanced technology. These exiled Chinese became and continued to become a source of technological secrets for the Chinese.

In more recent years, Chinese political contributions enhanced the spy gathering capabilities of Chinese agents, scientists and industrialists. The Chinese Secret Service appealed to loyalties and family ties and not financial bribes or sexual favors. Family ties and ancestor obligations date back thousands of years and are well ingrained in the Chinese psyche. Some Chinese scientists were lured back to the homeland by the appeal to obligatory responsibilities and others were left in place for future needs. There was a mass defection of Chinese scientists, but the Chinese Secret Service kept its network in the United States, intact at all levels.

The changes in US immigration laws facilitated the migration of Chinese by the tens of thousands, most settling on the West Coast.

Overseas Chinese agents also developed a corresponding relationship with American-Chinese scientists at meetings, through periodicals and scientific journals. These relationships have become both professional-scientific and personal.

Without question China has been able to develop almost faultless coordination between its military, political, scientific and intelligence people. Chinese intelligence activities operate within a legal framework and are 'low key'. The Chinese appeal to familial and family loyalty rather than strong-arm tactics. The methods of intelligence collection are so variable and utilize the facilities of so many organizations that intelligence operatives do not appear unique or stand out in any way. They are part and parcel of the fabric of American society.

China has also been assisted by the sale of technology by 'friendly' U.S. allies. An example of this is the sale of classified communications technology by Israel to China, which enabled the Chinese to monitor aircraft transmissions in International waters.

Susan Lee had developed a close friendship with Yeah Chun, a Chinese-American woman working at *Letni* and David Wong the lead person 'upstairs', where Susan sometimes worked. Kwang Lee and 'Joe' Park, two Korean born scientists were also part of this small 'clique'.

Friendships based on ethnic and national characteristics were not unusual at *Letni* and no one gave a second thought to such associations.

It was David who appealed to Susan's Chinese identification. She had helped him on a number of occasions and became a courier of software and hardware documents between departments. The advantage she had was the necessity of mobility as part of her job as she moved freely from one department to another.

Without mistake, however, she recognized a sinister perhaps cruel side to David's personality. He, in turn, had come to trust her.

David was a Chinese agent 'in place' whose 'control' in Beijing had researched Susan's background, at least as far as it went. There were gaps to be sure, but her birth, education and family background were impeccably detailed in the Secret Service report along with a history of family relationships. Her parents were born in Harbin, China and were of the 'old school'. Briefly stated, Susan was a perfect "target" to become a 'friendly'.

David exploited her Chinese background whenever he could and also emphasized the commonalties rather than differences with their Asian Korean brothers.

Kwang Lee and 'Joe' Park did not openly discuss politics but Susan was aware of their longing for a unified Korea.

Shortly after the death of Dieter Zook, David approached Susan for a 'favor', explaining in some detail how important it was to obtain documents and possibly other information that was now likely in the possession of Jason Knox, attorney at law.

Susan readily accepted the 'assignment' and awaited further instructions from David.

How much the others in this clique were privy to David's concerns remained to be seen.

Several days had passed since the ransacking of Jason's office and condo.

Paul Howieson telephoned Jason several times regarding the events, asking if he had any further information or if anything further had happened and again tried to engage his services.

Jason did not want to be used and he tried to 'brush off' Paul as politely as possible. In reality he hoped the whole situation would die out.

The question was what to do with the documents Zook had passed on and what risk would there be in retrieving them. After some legal research Jason decided to retrieve the materials and pass them on to Paul.

Hopefully, without the documents this would end his involvement in this scenario.

He drove to the U.S. Bank on Broadway, where he had a safe deposit box. After about thirty minutes in the vault he left and drove to the offices of Kolb, Alder and Rubenstein, where he rented vault storage space.

The vault secretary was out for a few hours and so he was not able to gain access to his drawer. Security at the firm was tight and only the senior partners and the vault custodian, could let him in.

He deposited the contents of his briefcase in an outer locked section of the vault and decided to go across the street for a sandwich and a cup of coffee.

The elevator door opened in the lobby. Jason noticed the sun coming through the double doors and thought about the weekend and of asking Greta to take a drive to the coast on Friday. He could finish up early and this would be a great time to reassure her about her safety and the events of the past few weeks.

Thus absorbed in his own reverie he felt a sense of warmth on his right side and then a hard shove. The warmth turned to heat and as he grabbed his side. He felt wet and sticky. Stunned, he turned and faced a small, nondescript man who was by this time in front of him holding a bloody knife and grabbing his briefcase.

"Give me the fucking case!"

Jason was catapulted forward and whether by choice or not he released the briefcase.

His assailant ran off case in arms.

Standing stunned Jason began to feel the wetness down his entire right side.

A bystander had gone into an adjacent bank and summoned the security guard.

Within minutes he found himself in the emergency room of Good Samaritan Hospital. The E.R. doctor was bending over him as two nurses mopped and cleansed his wounds.

"You're lucky. One laceration has gone through your love handle and the other seared part of your triceps. Didn't go through though."

Jason didn't appreciate the humor and what's more did not consider himself lucky.

"Doesn't look like any internal organs are damaged but I want to keep you for observation. We'll need some lab studies and X-rays as well. If all goes well I could release you sometime tonight."

Jason grunted. He was in no position to negotiate his treatment. He was truly shaken.

"How about that? Mugged in broad daylight. Did they get much?"

"It was a 'he'," Jason responded, "and he took my briefcase."

With this comment Jason remembered that his briefcase was almost empty. Other than his weekly calendar, a calculator and some miscellaneous, easily replaceable legal papers, nothing of material value was lost.

The damage to Jason's pride and sense of security were beginning to sink in when the police arrived.

Both the security man and the doctor had notified the police and who should walk in but none other than

Detective Alexander.

"Well...hello Sir! Got something you'd like to tell me? Saw your name on the 911 dispatch. Couldn't miss it. You're a known figure now...ransacked office, ransacked condo, knife attack. What next? You oughta join the marines. Be a lot safer. At least you could shoot back."

Jason was speechless.

"Wanta tell me what this is about?"

"I don't really know. I have to think about it," replied Jason.

"You do that Sir. You do that. When you're ready I'll take a statement. But don't wait too long. You might not be so lucky next time. Way I see it you got somethin' somebody else wants. Common sense. Detective sense. Any idea what that is?"

Jason nodded his head.

"O.K. have it your way. I do homicide too. Know what we say? 'My day begins when your days end,' that's our motto."

Jason did not appreciate the humor especially since the pain medication he had been given was starting to wear off and he felt the ache in his side and arm.

He hoped Alexander would simply disappear.

The nurse came in and gave Jason injections of an antibiotic and Demerol.

A few hours later he was in a light sleep when Greta arrived. He woke instantly as she approached his side.

"How did you know I was here?"

"That policeman, Alexander, called the office and told me you had been stabbed. He asked a lot of questions. There wasn't much I could tell him though. I called the hospital right away and the doctor said your wounds were 'not fatal'. I love the sense of humor they have around here. Anyway, I rushed over. You *are* lucky and this was no coincidence or accident. You're coming home with me for a few days. Then maybe we can talk about what's going on. When you feel better. And, Oh, Mr. Howieson called. Seems that Alexander and he had a chat. Mostly he wanted to see if I was O.K."

At this moment it dawned on Jason that Greta might be in danger of people trying to get to him.

The drugs and the pain clouded his thinking and he had little response other than to follow Greta's directives.

For the next few days Greta changed his bandages, fed him and saw to it that he took his medicines. Jason was a good patient and did what he was told. Greta 'covered' the office and made appropriate excuses for his absence. Negative publicity would not do for the success of his practice and now she had her own stake in things. She had also become fiercely loyal and personally involved in his life. Yet...a distance between them remained. Perhaps, an unbridgeable distance.

Who could tell? Do we ever really know someone? Where does individuality end and fusion begin? Greta was a student of Carl Jung and believed in the collective unconscious as well as the blending of universal human experience. We are all interconnected, one-way or another. Thus, the ultimate reality of existence was elusive and non consequential.

It had been some time since she studied Soren Kierkegaard but she lived, and not just studied, philosophy. This perspective lent itself well to the relationship she had with Jason and the sharing of her views and advice.

Jason in turn exposed himself emotionally and openly discussed his vulnerability. He described what he knew about Dieter Zook, Zooks sister Elisabett Hansberger and Paul Howieson. He spoke about his past, the life he left behind in Eastern Europe and ultimately of Sophie.

Greta stood, listening intently, tearfully. Feeling a deep warmth, she reached for his hand closing it into hers.

Jason rose and gently nudged her against the wall. He kissed her on the lips then the neck. His lips snuggled her ear and his hands undid the clasp on her dress, which smoothly, quietly, fell to the floor. Jason undid her bra, cupped his hands on her smooth breasts and, feeling her erect nipples, moved his hands to her waist gradually removing her panties. She simultaneously slid his pajama bottoms off and he entered the warmth and depth of her. She raised her arms momentarily as if to become part of the wall, then pulling his head to her bosom, she climaxed. Her legs tightly gripped his waist as he thrust ever harder and reached his peak. They slid down on the matted carpet and lay motionless for an eternity.

Greta hugged him ever so closely. She spoke first: "You're a strange man, Mr. Knox."

"How so?"

"The way you stare at me sometimes."

Jason tried to laugh off the comment: "I like your Victoria's secret panties."

"No. It's as if you're looking through me or into me or maybe seeing another person when you look at me."

Jason was clearly uncomfortable with this line of thinking and did not respond.

"I don't understand you and your eyes are a mystery. I can't see into them the way I want to."

He responded: "I see," and this sounded stupid.

With his clearly cold comment Greta stood, picked up her clothes and went into the bathroom.

Jason felt like a child. He pulled up his pajamas, stretched out on the sofa and feeling abandoned, closed his eyes.

Greta was with him when he telephoned the FBI.

Together they had decided that Jason had no choice but to cooperate with the Feds. Whoever was after him had by this time realized that they did not get what they wanted. His life was in continuous danger and so was Greta's.

Howieson suggested that Jason meet with him alone and that Greta keep as low a profile as possible. Howieson arranged for and FBI agent to accompany Jason.

At least they were all in agreement about this.

In the company of the FBI agent, Jason retrieved the Zook documents at the Kolb, Alder and Rubenstein law firm.

The meeting took place at the Pittock Building and not at the Federal building. The government rented space in this building. Security was tight and, more importantly, meeting in a nondescript office was low profile.

The office they met in on the third floor had no outside markings or identification of any kind other than a number.

Jason knocked and was immediately let in.

The space contained a few office chairs, a table and a video monitor.

Paul greeted him enthusiastically and motioned him to a chair opposite two men who were likely FBI agents.

Jason taking all of this in, soon noticed a uniformed marine sergeant sitting off to one side.

Paul spoke first. "I'd like you to meet Sergeant Brensen. Jason, Sergeant. Sergeant, Jason.

"Sir," respond the marine. "Happy to meet you, Sir."

"Likewise," responded Jason somewhat taken aback. He hadn't expected the marines to have landed.

"Sergeant Brensen will be your shadow in the days to come. I'll explain a little of what needs to be done and your 'need to know' as we say in the business."

Jason was familiar with the 'need to know' routine. It meant he would be told only part of the story. Maybe not even half the story. But then again maybe the less he knew the better. The safer?

Still...he liked to be in control. He wanted to know the whole story.

Knowing full well he would be kept in the dark about much of what was going on he didn't ask questions.

The FBI regarded Jason as a hero-a man of character, and a man who would never let his country down.

Paul knew that for Jason, honor wasn't everything, it was the 'only' thing. He also sensed that Jason, in his heart, had never left intelligence work. For Paul, and the policy planners at FBI Headquarters, Jason was not in a victim profile. They regarded him as a man who would become empowered the moment he grasped his place in this drama.

In history, so to speak. He was being welcomed, indeed sought after, as a main player on the team.

His sense of duty clearly marked him as a 'reliable' and a man who would put his life on the line. His past life experience demonstrated this already.

He had held up under intense interrogation and confinement by Czech authorities. CIA profilers assured the FBI that this character structure would prevail in the future.

Jason listened and listened and listened.

Paul had a fair amount to say.

Jason was indeed in significant danger and he was going on a trip. It was best if Greta left town as well. Sergeant Brensen would help Jason with arrangements. Would even pack for him if he wanted him to.

Jason couldn't even go to the bathroom without the sergeant being close by.

Jason noticed that the marine was armed.

They left the building separately. The sergeant followed in an unmarked Ford sedan.

About the same time, in Hillsboro, Susan Lee was telling her friends at the *Letni* Corporation about an upcoming vacation to her favorite resort in Sun River, Oregon.

What a piece of work is man!…in form and moving how express and admirable! In action how like an angel!

Shakespeare
Hamlet III,2

SEVEN

SERGEANT BRENSEN

Jason drove to Greta's home before going to his condo.

He knew she would be there and he wanted to tell her what he knew and say goodbye.

Brensen pulled up behind him. Jason was already beginning to feel the pressure of being watched...and pushed. He didn't like it.

Greta was casually dressed in shorts and a cotton sweater and was milling through some paper work spread out on her dining room table.

The sprinkles of rain had by now turned into a steady stream of clouds darkening the afternoon sky.

He spoke briefly about the meeting explaining the need for leaving town. He told her that an FBI agent had been assigned to accompany her as her safety was everyone's greatest concern.

She said she would go to stay with her parents for a time.

They talked of seeing one another again as soon as Jason returned from wherever he was going.

Feeling frightened, Greta blurted out "please don't tell me you are in love, what if I never see you again?"

"With men, springtime is one thing. November another. Ardor and temperature are inversely proportional."

This sounded pedantic but it helped her deal with the separation.

She was smiling-perhaps joking now. "I'll see you long before November and....I'll be in touch..."

He was in no mood for jokes. In fact, Jason was experiencing a deep sense of dread and emptiness. He was totally off balance and in emotional pain.

Greta knew this. She tried to reassure him by making some remarks about putting the office in order and responding to calls via voice mail. She assured Jason of some continuity in the practice and, of course, he could access the system from wherever he might be. It would be as if he were in town.

They hugged, kissed and said goodbye. Jason walked to his car, turned briefly and waved and drove off, feeling lost.

Sergeant Brensen was close behind.

Jason packed, locked some things away for safe keeping, not that it mattered at this point. He threw his stuff on the rear seat and climbed into Brensen's Ford.

"Where we going?"

"North, Sir."

"Where North?"

Silence followed. Jason soon learned that the silences meant that Sergeant Brensen did not wish to respond. For the most part the sergeant was inscrutable.

Soon they were on I-5 headed north toward Seattle.

Jason wondered where and hoped maybe Seattle. Seattle had great restaurants and he liked being around the water.

Brensen's behavior was understated. He spoke

little, volunteered nothing and seemed to have no opinions.

When they stopped for a rest break at a truck stop the sergeant reservedly kept an eye on him. Face to face Jason looked over his ribbons that included among others the Vietnam Air Medal, a Silver Star with Oak Leaf Cluster and a Purple Heart.

Brensen had served two tours of duty in 'Nam and Jason could barely make out the burn scars around his neck. No doubt his uniform covered the remainder. Jason guessed the sergeant was a casualty of a rocket attack. He would be no one to fool with and no one's fool. Jason respected that.

Nevertheless, he could not resist asking the question and tried to be funny about it. "You got a first name Sarge?"

A long silence followed and Jason felt stupid and awkward for having asked.

Finally..."Yes sir," the sergeant replied dutifully.

Jason waited but no further comment was forthcoming. "What is it," he blurted out, wanting to finish this scenario of verbal fencing. A long silence followed.

"Matthew, sir."

Jason considered and then thought better than to ask this man if he could call him Matt or Matthew. In his own mind he settled for sergeant and that would be that.

"Thank you, sergeant."

"Yes sir."

Jason got the message and stopped asking questions.

About ten minutes later the sergeant's spontaneous comments surprised Jason.

"We're on a mission, sir. A serious professional mission."

By this comment Jason understood that this was not a social relationship. This was not a vacation. This was not a day off in the life of Sergeant Matthew Brensen.

The FBI had found it necessary to have him protected by an experienced combat marine. A man who would risk his own life to protect the mission-to protect Jason. A man who was already tested, tried and true. A part of American history.

He thought of the marines he had met, who had been part of the Chosen Reservoir Campaign. They were 'walking history'. It also became strikingly clear that his life was up for grabs.

Jason's arm still ached, although it was healing. His hip was sore around the beltline but, otherwise fine and he was no longer taking pain medicine. He thought of the flippant comment the doctor had made-"love handle." He started to drift off to sleep. For the first time in weeks he was beginning to relax.

A sleep of dreams ensconced his being and Jason found himself walking through a fragrant meadow bathed in sunshine and flowers. He awakened to find that Brensen had turned off onto 101 and was just pulling in to a truck stop south of Shelton, Washington.

"Time for a break, Sir."

Jason reluctantly gave up the meadow and went inside for a cup of coffee.

Within minutes that seemed like seconds the sergeant was at his table in mufti, his uniform in a small canvas bag by his side.

"From here on in we tone things down. No need to invite comment."

Jason ordered a sandwich, his companion a burger and a cup of coffee and soon they were on their way. Passing thru Potlatch, Hoodsport, Eldon, Brinnon and Seal Rock they both seemed to be taking in the beauty of the area.

At Quilcene he wondered if they were going to turn off towards Port Angeles or back down 104 towards Bremerton. They seemed to be getting further and further away from any military installation.

He kept his own counsel. He enjoyed the vistas of the Olympic Mountains off to the left and glimpses of Rainier to the East. The Hood Canal with its deep and fast moving waters had a beauty all its own and the entire area seemed to Jason to be elusive, wild and undiscovered, a land of beauty and interest. He was absorbing the natural beauty.

About twenty-five miles northward a sign announced that they were entering Port Townsend.

They turned up Blaine Street as Jason feasted his eyes on the turn of the century designed Victorian homes. Reaching Johnson Street the sergeant turned left and parked on an off road spot.

"Let's go."

"Where are we going?"

"Let's go.

Jason should have learned by now that his questions were redundant.

They walked a few feet to the right and approached the beautifully carved sign that announced with not a little dignity: 'CHETZEMOKA PARK'. They walked past the gazebo on the left towards a park bench overlooking Admiralty Bay Inlet. The sun was shining now and the view was astoundingly beautiful. They sat in silence surrounded by flowers.

The sergeant's side arm was visible from beneath the cotton sweater he had changed into. He seemed nervous and his eyes darted around.

A woman with two small children milled around the gazebo. They wandered toward the bench. The woman came over, swooped the children by the arms and softly stated: "They are waiting for you." She disappeared almost as quickly as she had arrived.

"It's all clear, let's go."

They returned to the car.

A short drive later and they entered an area known as Fort Worden State Park. The large grassy parade ground is lined on each side with handsome Victorian houses. The homes along Officers' Row had all been restored.

After entering the park, the sergeant drove by Officer' Row then doubled back and pulled into an area behind the houses.

Jason noticed that the cars in the area had Department of Defense parking decals on the rear windows.

Brensen motioned him inside a two story non-descript building. Inside on each side of the doorway were two men carrying weapons Jason recognized as H&K MP5's. His fear again emerged. This was indeed serious.

A voice echoed from a darkened back room and a figure moved forward.

"Welcome to Fort Worden and our 'safe house'. There are some people I'd like you to meet." It was Paul, dressed Army fatigues. A .45 caliber sidearm rested on his belt.

Paul introduced a man he addressed as Mr. Berger from Washington D. C. He was the Director's representative and seemed friendly enough through his officious manner.

"Coffee?"

"Sure. I'll have a cup."

Jason turned to include Sergeant Brensen in the conversation but the marine was nowhere to be found.

"Please sit down, we have a lot to go over."

Paul's goal, 'The Mission' so to speak, was to intercept the flow of intelligence information to countries inimical to the best interests of the United States, to plant false information in the hands of enemy agents (disinformation) and eventually, when advantageous to expose foreign counter intelligence agents in place. This would have to be at the most opportune moment.

With Jason's last mission he had lost the love of his life, would he have to choose again between honor and duty and lose Greta in the process or might he have both? This seemed to be his internal psychological dilemma, at least at the moment.

After about fifteen minutes of preliminaries and discussion of the importance of the mission and its secret nature, Paul asked one of the guards to summon the next visitor.

"Hi, come on in," Paul boomed as a young woman was escorted into the room.

Jason feasted his eyes on a slender, lithe Asian woman with slanted eyes and Raven jet-black hair. Her high cheekbones added to an attractively sculptured face that bordered on the beautiful. Jason was breathless as the young woman spoke softly and quietly:

"It's nice to meet you, Mr. Knox. I'm Susan."

Paul went on to explain that Susan Lee was a deep cover agent who had spent the last few years of her life infiltrating an espionage ring at the *Letni* Corporation. She was the equivalent of what the enemy might call a 'cut out', someone leading a seemingly normal life while in the employ of a secret government agency. In this case, the United States. She worked a routine job and had an average life.

All Jason could think of was that Susan did not

look like a Susan. She was stunning. He was not only breathless, he was also speechless.

"Did you have difficulty providing a cover story to leave Letni?" Howieson asked.

"No, I announced plans to vacation at Sun River Resort.

Those about her
From her shall read the perfect ways of honor.

Shakespeare
Henry VIII, V,5

EIGHT

SUSAN

Susan took charge as Paul excused himself. "I'll leave you in the able hands of Susan, she'll explain what we're doing here."

Jason quickly thought he'd like to be in Susan's hands as she motioned him into an adjacent room where he followed dutifully.

They both sat down in straight back chairs next to a large table. Losing himself for a moment he briefly thought of Greta as he realized an attraction for Susan.

Susan's life had not had not been easy. Her mother opposed her interest in law enforcement and expressed the typical Chinese distrust of the police. Charlie Chan not withstanding, Susan's mother Tzu-hsi was adamant in her protests. She wanted her daughter to marry a "vely nice China boy. A docta'. Have baby. House. Be prospa'. Susan was determined and the more her mother pushed, the more she resisted.

As a young woman she found her contemporaries jealous of her attractiveness, although she was far from being flirtatious with men. In jeans, high heels and lipstick she was stunning. On occasion she wore traditional Chinese smocks, lightly adorned with a gold medallion given to her by her father as a good luck charm. At work she dressed down and wore no makeup or jewelry.

The women at the FBI Academy were no less charitable in their behavior towards her. Susan's rectitude and penchant for detachment from social frivolity was mistaken for arrogance and an 'I'm better than you' attitude. Nothing was further from the truth as Susan longed to identify with her new culture and be 'American'.

Likely her desire to join the FBI had its roots in this desire, as the Bureau stood for Americana and was, in her mind, a national symbol.

While the men agents in training gawked at her, the women dubbed her "Suzie Wong" or "The Dragon Lady." She became the object of pranks and locker room gossip. Nevertheless she persevered, graduating at the top of her class with special recognition.

At graduation she was given the App Award for excellence with firearms.

Her assignments, partly by choice and partly by need involved the political sector of Bureau work. As a Chinese-American she fit in where others did not.

Among other assets, she had a pilot's license, was a certified diver and excelled in martial arts; especially Kung Fu and Tai Chi. She had some experience with Japanese Kendo, Karate and Korean Taek Won Do.

Susan's eyes penetrated Jason, as she explained how close Portland's ties were with Taiwan. She was providing some background so he could understand the Chinese community. Portland's sister city for eleven years had been Kaohsiung and the relationship expanded form the cultural and educational one to the economic arena with the visit of Kaohsiung's mayor, Frank Chang-ting Hsieh to Portland.

Jason finally regained his composure and, not wishing to appear ignorant, mumbled something about the Dragon Boat Races and the exchange program with young women from Shu Te High School as examples of Chinese-Portland connections.

Susan nodding agreement also mentioned the U.S. China-People's Friendship Association with its emphasis on Mainland China rather than Taiwan. The organization had, over the years, sponsored many trips to China and some to Tibet.

Jason listened intently.

Susan explained her work at *Letni* and described her Asian co-workers from her perspective as an undercover agent.

Jason began to understand that he was to be a go between in the passage of information to the Chinese.

"They already think you are involved," explained Susan, "so we might as well play along with it."

Jason didn't like the word "play."

"Besides, she explained, "you already received sensitive information that was passed on to you by Zook."

The more Susan spoke the more Jason realized she was not just a perfunctory in this operation. She was one of the planners.

"By the way, so who was it that tossed my office and condo? The FBI?"

She did not respond but went on the explain the need for *humint* - human intelligence and operatives, but he already understood the lingo and background of operations. He was, nevertheless, impressed with her knowledge and professionalism.

Susan, Suzie Wong, Dragon Lady was winning his admiration as well as his mind. She attracted him sexually and physically but, he was not fully aware of his sexual feelings.

Susan continued. She explained the Chinese appeal to patriotism and use of guilt in recruiting agents.

She understood the guilt technique well but didn't discuss her personal life with Jason. She explained that American's are recruited, by foreign intelligence agencies, with financial bribes, and the English with sexual favors.

Jason knew all of this but found himself cast in a spell as he listened to Susan's sometimes singsong voice. She had never fully discarded the tonal variations of her native language and Jason was enjoying every minute of it.

He was briefed on the principals involved, shown photographs of people and places and given a pretty good idea of the purpose of the mission.

After she finished, Paul joined them for a light lunch of sandwiches and soup served in a carton container.

Jason asked the whereabouts of the sergeant and was told that he would be staying at the Harborside Inn.

Jason would be spending the next few days on Fort Worden. Although the Harborside was secure, foreign intelligence could eavesdrop on conversations using microwave transmissions, especially through windows. In fact the CIA had developed a technique to record conversations after individuals left the room. The technique involved 'capturing' the sound waves that were still present and using a device to organize them into meaningful speech patterns. Paul explained that Fort Worden would be safer. Technology had come a long way!

The remainder of the day was spent sightseeing in the Port Townsend vicinity. Paul wanted Jason to be as relaxed as possible for the briefings that were to follow and he also wanted this to look like a vacation trip.

Paul assigned an FBI secretary to accompany Jason on his walks through town. She was happy to leave the steno pool and proved to be a nice conversationalist especially regarding the geography of the area.

She talked of the Rhododendron Festival, the Victorian architecture, Old Fort Townsend State Park, the old U.S. Army post built in 1856 to protect the early settlers and how is had been turned into a wildlife sanctuary.

Perhaps more importantly the town had an almost magical feel. A place to get out of a rut, to slow down, a place to absorb the serenity.

Jason, for a moment forgot the danger and intrigue of the past few months as his eyes feasted on a fairytale castle like building that combined Romanesque and Gothic idioms.

"What's that bell tower", he asked thinking of the eclectic architectural contributions.

"That's the courthouse, it was built in 1892. The 100-foot clock tower is a mariners' homing landmark. Come, let me show you St. Pauls Church, it was built in 1865 and is the oldest Episcopal church in the diocese of Olympia. And, the bell…donated by a cutter captain on the condition that it be rung on foggy days to guide sailing ships into the bay."

Jason ended up hearing a little more about fly-fishing than he really wanted to but coffee at the Silverwater Cafe was a delight.

Afterward they walked over to Union Wharf and after browsing though some book shops, the secretary drove him back to Fort Worden. They agreed on a time for dinner.

Jason was shown to his room by one of the guards he had previously met. Although tired after his hot shower he felt stimulated. The excitement of the "old days" was with him again. They say "once a spy, always a spy."

In 1885, George Sterming erected a building that

houses the famous Belmont Restaurant and Saloon. Sterming catered to the maritime trade, offering good food, strong whiskey and a party-like atmosphere. His customers included sea captains, cargo brokers, adventurers and runners, gamblers and hustlers, all interacting amid cigar smoke and occasional pandemonium. The Belmont today is Port Townsend's only remaining 1880's waterfront restaurant and saloon.

Dorothy, the secretary and Jason had dinner in the courtyard and savored after dinner drinks. She paid the bill with a "company" credit card, drove Jason back to the Fort early, as she had been instructed. Tomorrow she would be back in the typing pool.

Shortly after falling asleep Jason was awakened to receive a telephone call from Greta. She had been given the number of an alleged Seattle law firm, which was a "cover", and the call was put through to Paul and then Jason.

After a few preliminaries and questions about what Jason might be doing, Greta explained that she was returning to Portland. She wanted to keep working and the FBI had assured her of around the clock protection. Work in the office was piling up and her Germanic background was coming into play.

Although she didn't say it, she missed Jason and hoped he would say he missed her.

He did not, even though his heart yearned for her. After all, the line was probably tapped. No time for sentimentality. Jason thanked her for the call.

Lying back in bed he began thinking of her cotton white laced panties and drifted off to sleep.

The smell of bacon and eggs permeated everything as Jason awoke. A Filipino cook was downstairs in the kitchen and after a relatively brief breakfast with Paul, Jason was introduced to two nondescript scientist types. He dubbed one "Mr. Peepers" and the other "Computer Nerd." Mr. Peepers was from NASA and Computer Nerd from NSA, the super secret government communications agency.

Jason was aware that a major NSA listening post was located in Washington State. These men were not unlike the cryptographic civilian types he had met at tracking stations throughout the world during the Viet Nam War. Paul and the supervisors in The Capitol wanted Jason to know as much of the technical side as possible. After all, he was supposed to know what he was passing back and fourth. There wasn't much time, and Jason and the scientists worked in two hour rotating shifts with brief coffee breaks in between. They covered cryptography, missile guidance systems, directional plotting, propulsion and tracking. Very few in this section knew that many of the scientific secrets were being stolen already, some by political and financial bribery and others by intimidation. There were leaks at the highest levels of government as well as the government's research laboratories like the one at Los Alamos. The Chinese had done a good job with their "ping pong diplomacy," wushu martial arts, exchange students and cultural performances in lulling the American public into a state of complacency. Even embassies, American Embassies, even the one in Washington D.C., had been 'bugged'.

The Chinese and North Koreans already had major missile technology that threatened American cities. Only the military and security agencies were attuned to what was happening but in a democracy were powerless to intervene. Influential politicians in Washington looked to China for financial and political support. Top Brass military experts believed some top Administration officials were selling them down the drain.

There was little verbal interaction between Jason and the two scientists. He was talked "at" rather than talked "to".

His thoughts frequently drifted to Greta. He wondered where she was and when he would see her again. All in all he was happy when this section of his briefing was over.

Dorothy, who had spent the better part of the day in the typing pool, picked him up at the prearranged time of seven and they dined on fish at the *Surf Restaurant*. Both were tired and it was an early night.

Jason dreamt of mathematical formulas and statistics. In his dreams he tried to put things together but tossed and turned in confusion.

The third day was spent learning a little about Chinese dissident groups, writers and Chinese religious history.

A professor from the University of Washington briefed Jason on *dissident* religious groups. He learned about the second-century *Yellow Turbans* whose Taoist clergy led the rebellion against the Han Dynasty, the *White Lotus Sect* whose members expelled the Mongols in the 13th century, the *Christian* influenced Taiping Rebellion in the mid-19th century that left millions dead across China, the late 19th century *Boxers* the xenophobic group that held foreigners hostage in Beijing, the *Unity Sect* of the 1940's and 50's banned by the Communists and im-portantly the *Falun Dafa* with its exercise regimen of quiet contemplation. *The White Lotus Sect* and *Falun Dafa* along with cults and secret societies are flourishing in an era of lost values and challenging and unnerving leaders. Jason learned that these organizations borrow heavily from Taoist, Buddhist and Confucian traditions and have been able to traditionally challenge the government in China and occasionally topple authority. The government's response is to have these groups banned and recently Falun Dafa has had to go underground. With its well organized hierarchy headed by Li Hingzhi the Chinese government believed its authority was seriously threatened. Falfun Dafa had refused to register with the government in a pledge of loyalty and ignored the Communist demand that its *qi gong* exercises be "scientific." Mao himself believed qi gong to be too meditative and spiritual. In short, not active enough and too much of a threat. The possibility of politization and violence, although dormant, was not acceptable to the present regime. The possibility of 100 million members worldwide is upsetting to the powers that be in China. Even with the ban Falun Dafa has kept up its defiant stance, while the military and police were warned against involvement and urged to "educate" people against it. At least 100 of the group's leaders had been arrested along with other members and some had disappeared shortly before Jason was being briefed.

He took all of this in stride, but was developing some degree of information overload. Paul understood this and the day's briefing ended by 2PM.

There followed a walk on the beach by the light-house and a picturesque sunset.

"I'm about done in," Jason commented to Paul who had been unusually quiet. "Tired and saturated."

"A boat ride tomorrow and a change of scene will do you some good, Knox. I guarantee you'll have a good time. Practical...know what I mean."

Jason wasn't sure what he did mean but let the comment pass. For the first time in weeks, perhaps months, he felt good about himself.

Back in his room Jason was unable to sleep.

Pacing about his room, his mind retracing the day, he picked up a brochure and began to read.

"Fort Worden State Park encompassing 444 acres, a coastal fortress, guarding the entrance to Puget Sound during Theodore Roosevelt's presidency. The Hong Kong of the Washington Park System and a role model across the nation. A fort built to protect our nation's freedoms. Now a place to practice and exercise those freedoms..."

"The Puget Sound Harbor Defense System included Forts Flagler on Marrowstone Island, Casey on Whidby Island and Worden in Port Townsend. The construction began in 1897 and Fort Worden became the system headquarters. It had the most modern concrete gun emplacement and fire control methods of its time. The military lowered its flags at For Worden in 1953 and in 1972 Washington State Parks Commission turned the facility into a multi-use conference center. Fort Worden had guarded the entrance to Admiralty Inlet through which any hostile fleet must pass to reach such prime targets as the Bremerton Navy Yard..."

Jason sensed he was part of the web of history. He had a purpose, he felt needed. He realized that he was here for another kind of government, perhaps akin to the original purpose of the fort. That fit with the noble history of this place.

He sensed what the Navajo's called Harmony. Harmony before me, harmony behind me, harmony beside me. He slept well that night.

There are more things in heaven and earth, Horatio,
Than are dreamt of in your philosophy.

Shakespeare
Hamlet I,5

NINE

CHUCK

Paul's comment was an understatement. The ferry ride was more than a good time. It was an experience in living for the moment.

Brensen was by his side the entire trip and, after parking the car below deck, Jason insisted they remain top deck. He stood at the rail the entire trip taking in the broad vistas of Puget Sound and the magnificent beauty surrounding him. The departing view of Port Townsend gave him a generous understanding of the environs and the tiered geography of the city.

Within about 15 minutes fog set in and soon deepened, Jason thought this very romantic and that thought led to fantasies of Greta and then of Susan and then of Greta until his reveries were interrupted by the loud fog horn warning any boaters of the accompanying vessel.

By now Jason knew enough to not ask questions but he wasn't surprised when they pulled up to Whidbey Island. As if by magic the sun appeared brightening the ferry port entrance.

Captain George Vancouver discovered Whidbey Island in 1792 and named it after Joseph Whidbey his sailing master. He proved the island was not a peninsula by navigating Deception Pass. The bridge over the pass has a complicated history and it was not until 1934 that construction was begun. In less than a year the cantilevered spans were ready to be joined but steelworkers were unable to align the two sections connecting Whidbey with Fidalgo Island. In the cool of the morning, however, the metal had contracted enough to allow proper matching of the diagonals and the joining was completed. Deception Pass was bridged. Whidbey is the largest island in Puget Sound and contains much farmland, forest and scenic shoreline with magnificent vistas. The town of Coupeville is one of the oldest towns in the state and not only offers attractive bay views but is charming and serene. Langley is a picturesque town with a historic atmosphere. Oak Harbor, the largest town on the island, is junky and unattractive. The buildings, farms, military fortifications and overall milieu afford the visitor with a historical record of the area's exploration and settlement. The charm of this Island is intoxicating.

The sergeant spoke first. "We have time to kill. Let's get some breakfast."

"Fine with me," responded Jason, who, by this time in the open air had built up a hearty appetite.

Brensen knew exactly where he was going and drove up highway 20 passing farmlands.

Jason noticed that outside one farmhouse a Chow sat like a statue quietly observing his surroundings and neither barking nor moving as they passed.

They breakfasted at the *Knead & Feed*, a quaint little place. The sign outside said it was established in 1974.

Brensen ordered pancakes and eggs and Jason ordered 'The Italian', a three-egg omelet with sausage. The portions were large by any standards and complimented by broad views of Penn Cove and The Saratoga Passage beyond.

By this time Jason was caught up in the excitement and mystery of the moment. His life was becoming a real adventure. He sensed that his law practice in Portland would never be the same and felt uneasy about this. He was caught up not only in the mystery of the moment but the sense of purpose that seemed to him to blend in with the natural beauty of his surroundings.

On the trip to Port Townsend the Olympic Mountains reigned on the West side and Mt. Rainier dominated the east with so much varied landscape in between. The magic of the experience had become cumulative and he was sensing himself as being, in the Buddhist sense, interwoven with the universe.

The sergeant suggested they spend some more time in town and led his charge to *The Mystery Bookshop*, an apropos title under the circumstances. They both sat in the large overstuffed easy chairs and browsed through the books on the side tables. They spent a few minutes at the *Great Times Coffee House*.

After about 30 minutes the duo was again heading north on highway 20. When they reached Oak Harbor, Jason was reminded of the ugliness of "auto row" in Beaverton, a small community outside Portland. By this time Jason surmised that the destination would most likely be the Naval Air Station and the Naval Reserve area, which turned out to be the case.

Brensen parked behind a nondescript wooden building that appeared as if it had been built during World War II. The sign outside read: "U.S. Navy. Quartermaster Supply." This turned out to be a misnomer. The building housed the Covert Operations Command station for a large section of the Northwest.

The Sergeant and Jason walked up the wooden steps and entered the building. Seated at a desk was a young woman who immediately looked up and stiffened in an alert posture. This Yeoman 1st class wore no lipstick or makeup. Her hair was brushed back and fastened in a bun giving her an overall constrained appearance. Jason thought she had that washed out look of a woman just getting out of bed in the morning. Yet...there was a simple, clean beauty and wholesomeness about this young woman.

In a sense there are two kinds of men in the world. Men who like woman and men who don't. Jason was one of those who loved women and everything they stood for. He thought women beautiful, which was surprising for a man who dated infrequently, had little interest in a permanent relationship and found work and reading more satisfying than social activities with the opposite sex.

This attractive Yeoman wore a heavily starched white uniform adorned with two rows of ribbons and a nametag that announced: "Owens."

Jason's manner could only be described as insouciant as he gazed upon her.

What he could not know and could not guess was her history-the personal story that all people have. The *story* that makes each person so unique and so interesting. The *story* behind the makeup, behind the flesh and sinew, behind the bone and nerves and blood vessels. The intangible sense of life and spirit.

Brenda Owens, Yeoman 1st class, United States Navy, was born in Morgantown, West Virginia. Her father died when she was 6 years old and she grew up with three older brothers and a mother who took in wash and sewing to help make ends meet. A mother who loved her dearly and brothers who protected her from the bullies at school. She was something of a "Tomboy" herself and by the time she reached junior high school she knew she was "different" than the other girls. Brenda was a natural for the Navy. She was active, athletic and understood men, having learned much from her brothers. She also needed a stabilizing, organizing force in her life.

Brenda joined the Navy right after high school and found what she needed. The Navy had been good for her and she had been good for the navy. Captain Taylor, her boss, ran interference for Brenda and took her under his wing. She needed protection from some of the bigots in the upper echelons of the Navy. She was a lesbian and followed the "Don't tell, don't ask" policy. True, as with the FBI, although the people at the top were changing their attitudes towards "minorities" and issues of sexual preference there were still the diehards and some of them could come down very hard. Taylor had become a father surrogate for Brenda and she in turn was fiercely loyal and protective of him and his mission statement.

The Yeoman stood up and her uniform crinkled. "Good morning. Good afternoon. I guess it's afternoon now." Ordinarily a quiet person, she recognized Brensen and was more forthcoming with her greeting.

"Hello sailor," responded Brensen who was surprisingly animated. "This is Jason Knox and we're here to see Captain Taylor."

As a security precaution and following proper Navy protocol and procedure Brenda asked to see the sergeants military identification once again as well as Jason's drivers license.

"Ah ha. O.K. Excuse me for a minute."

Brenda opened the adjacent door. "Sir, Sergeant

Brensen and Mr. Knox are here to see you sir."

A deep gravely voice responded: "Good, right on time and operationally ready. That's what I like. Send them in."

"Yes sir. You may go in now.

They entered a full sized room replete with wall maps, charts, books and a few photographs. A large mahogany table stood in the corner displaying stacks of documents and more photographs.

"Welcome aboard sergeant. Mr. Knox welcome to Flag Plot."

"Good afternoon Captain."

Upon hearing this Jason was immediately at ease. He knew he was welcome in this inner sanctum and that he wasn't just another task that had been piled on to this busy Captains work schedule. Jason knew that the Flag Plot is a small room where the plan of battle is laid out. A special place for Navy brass. It's called Flag Plot because it was built for admirals-"flags" to lay out their battle maps and charts and to plan strategy.

"Call me Chuck."

"O.K., call me Jason or Skip.

The Navy uses designators to identify skills and specialties. For example ship drivers are the 1100 series, security group types are 1610 et cetera. Chest badges also denote special qualifications such as flyers, submariners and Special Forces. Everyone wears stars above the stripes on the wrist except medical, dental chaplain and the lawyers. There is no special designation for intelligence officers. They like to hide. They also engage in less raillery than the average Naval officer.

Brenda knocked softly and brought in the coffee she knew the Captain expected. There were commissary bought cookies on a tray along with sugar but no cream. She left as quietly as she had come in.

Jason commented on her professionalism.

"She's a gem," Taylor responded. "Easy to get along with and very reliable. We need more like her in the Navy."

He did not discuss her personal life in any way.

For a moment after seeing the coffee Jason thought of Greta and how she always had brewed coffee waiting for him and his clients when he arrived at the office. He quickly put her out of his mind as he was girding for action. Taylor obviously had much to go over and the excitement of the moment was intoxicating. Jason did not want to miss a word.

After a few sips of coffee, Taylor put his cup down as did his companions as he motioned them over to the large table. They stood as the Captain rearranged some documents and pulled out some photographs.

Taylor spoke first: "Well gentlemen we'll start with the Array system." He went on to explain how the surveillance towed array system (SURTASS) was developed to overcome the disadvantages of the fixed SOSUS arrays. There followed a brief and relatively non-technical review of the rapidly deployable surveillance system and the ocean moored command actuated sonobuoys.

These as well as more advanced systems had now been linked to the FLATSATCOM - the fleet satellite communications system with on shore data processing facilities. This hardware and the data behind it had been prime targets for Red Chinese spies and this was continuing. The United States has the highest rate of submarine deployment of ballistic-missile submarines of any country in the world.

Taylor read from a document: *"The success or*

failure of deliberate, sustained strategic antisubmarine operations would be closely related to tactical antisubmarine force requirements, the control of waters adjacent to submarine-deployment areas and communications links with nuclear-powered attack submarines. Allied naval predominance in the deep-ocean basins has a potential wartime strategic significance greater than the substantial threat it presents to the enemy."

He went on to explain the need for the availability of accurate target information and how this was being developed. The work was parceled out to various laboratories on an expertise basis. Many of these labs were located in the Northwest.

The significance of this information was of utmost importance in the strategic balance with an adversary especially since it incorporated monitoring capabilities against an adversary. The ability to monitor the enemy was a stabilizing factor.

Jason could follow this very well. He had once boarded the USS Pogy in North Pacific waters during a storm. It was a harrowing experience but he understood some of the communications and Command Information Center needs of attack submarines.

A long time ago, almost in another life, he had been briefed about the Russian freighters with sophisticated electronic eavesdropping equipment that remained offshore to monitor Naval shipping especially submarines. A major northwest submarine base is located at Bangor, Washington near Tacoma.

What Taylor was explaining was that the Chinese had purchased homes in the surrounding areas to be used as "safe houses" and monitoring stations as they tracked and eavesdropped on the submarines in and out of Bangor. "The situation is even more complicated," Taylor explained. "In Khartoum of all places the Chinese Intelligence Service established close and unusual links with the French Intelligence in neighboring territories as well as with Israel. In the civil war that raged in Sudan these rival groups attempted to thwart and undermine one another for years. Following some of the hostilities China made a one hundred and fifteen million dollar interest-free loan to the Sudan. Chinese Intelligence nurtured its relationship with Israeli Intelligence in Khartoum to thwart Russian influence. This relationship has continued and Chinese and Israeli undercover agents make contact in this part of the world. That the Israeli's are on to the *Letni* secret research and development is a given. That the Chinese know the Israeli's are, is also a given. In Egypt at least one such double agent was a member of an Israeli Communist organization. This man eventually moved to the United States, lived incognito in San Francisco and ultimately disappeared."

Taylor went on to explain that the most secret of all organizations in the Chinese Secret Service is the Investigation Bureau. The basic structure of the Chinese Secret Service was reviewed including the Party Channel, the Central External Liaison Department, the State Council and the Military Intelligence Department. It is the C.E.L.D. that controls the various "Friendship" organizations.

All aspects of the Chinese Secret Service were operative in Portland. It has been specifically the *Cheng pao k'o*, or Political Security Section that has been responsible for counter-espionage operations. This section also controls the investigation of overseas Chinese. The *Chi pao k'o* or Organizational Security Section focuses its attention on personnel in government agencies, factories and universities.

With particular consideration to Susan the

Chinese were aware of double agents loyal to Taiwan. This legacy had developed from the Secret Service maintained by Chiang Kai-Shek. Interestingly Chinese who had returned to China from exile were given special privileges and recruited as spies.

Taylor went on and on and Jason's head was beginning to spin. He remembered Dorothy's fly-fishing 'lectures' at dinner in Port Townsend, only that was simple compared to this. Taylor was organized though and kept the technical material separate from the political realities.

Jason likened the Chinese double agent issue to Ellen Romach, a 27 year old. She was alleged to have had a very close personal relationship with JFK while working for the Communists in East Germany. Eventually the FBI investigated her. She was allegedly paid off and shipped back to Germany.

With the Chinese it was not so easy.

The briefing was interrupted when Brenda brought in sandwiches and salads.

Charles Taylor, code named Lewis, really knew his stuff. He was an admirer of Hyman Rickover and even worked with him for a time.

Rickover liked Taylor because of his thoroughness and nose to the grindstone attitude. He knew he could depend on him when the chips were down.

Taylor also became friends with J. Wilson Bradford who later became CINPAC - Commander In Chief Pacific and eventually one of the Joint Chiefs.

What Taylor would not confide to Jason were the attempts by Israeli and Chinese agents to procure data on the W-88 nuclear warhead that American scientists were developing. He had been ordered by both the Atomic Energy Commission and the Department of Defense that this was off limits for discussion. However, all involved parties knew that this project had been compromised by Chinese scientists working on the W-88 development and especially the computer simulation series.

They adjourned at 1630.

Jason wanted to have dinner at the *Captain Whidbey Inn*, but Taylor decided against it for security reasons. A meal was brought in on hot plates and Jason was taken to the BOQ, given some books and magazines and told to get a good nights rest.

That night he tried to scale the Great Wall of China but kept falling.

When awakened for breakfast at 'O dark hundred' he was hardly rested.

They were soon back at work in Taylor's office.

Today's review included material on the P-3 Orion aircraft that patrolled the offshore waters and the Navy's A-6 Intruder aircraft that had been involved in intelligence gathering and electronic countermeasures. The focus was on information obtained as well as the attempts of the Chinese to update their potential for these activities.

Things were looking up. Taylor announced that they were nearing the end of this briefing.

He knew Jason would be tired and Paul advised him to not overload his guest.

By late afternoon Brensen and Jason were crossing Deception Pass on their way to Anacortes. They spent the evening at the Ship Harbor Inn, sharing a cottage. Dinner this time was a treat and Brensen, obviously knowing his way around in a chow line took Jason to the *Compass Rose*, a surprisingly casual elegant Latin American restaurant. Dinner had been complimented with fine wines and Jason fell off to sleep quickly.

Brensen secured the perimeter as only a marine could do and they were both secure for the night. Brensen slept with his weapon close by his side.

In the morning they took highway 20 over to interstate 5 and thus south to Portland.

Jason thought he had had quite an adventure. Little did he know, it was just beginning.

Let Hercules himself do what he may,
The cat will mew, and the dog will have his day.

Shakespeare
Hamlet V,1

TEN

BOOK

The greatest influx of Italians into the United States occurred between the years 1880 to 1920. It reached an unprecedented peak from 1902 to 1914. Between 1887 and 1916, 3,984, 976 Italians arrived in the U.S., leaving their native environs not to seek political asylum but to support their families.

The overwhelming adversities of the southern agricultural regions of Italy, insufficient rainfall, obsolete farming methods, unrestrained deforestation, flooding, malaria, heavy taxes and usury, to name a few, rather than produce a mood of helplessness, led the Southern Italians to emigrate to provide for their families. Thus the immigrants were the most industrious Italy had to offer and more than half returned home when economic conditions improved.

American industrialists recognized that these Italians would provide a great labor pool, much as the railroad tycoons had with the Chinese 'coolies'. They sent agents with prepaid tickets to induce workers to come to the United States.

Thousands of Italians were employed as cheap labor on work gangs all over the country, especially on railroads. Work on the railroads brought Italians to Oregon. The climate and good farmland convinced them to stay. These people were, after all, farmers heart and soul.

Although the Oregon Board of Immigration Commission was created to induce foreigners to immigrate to the state, they favored Germans and Scandinavians. Sentiments were definitely anti-Italian, anti-Jew, anti-Chinese and anti-Catholic.

Once in Oregon, Italians worked for the railroads, in mills, lumber camps and on road construction, being offered less pay and poorer working conditions than indigenous workers. Italians were among Oregon's earliest pioneers and between 1844 and 1847 there were at least six Italian born pioneer-priests.

In the late 1840's, Antonio deMartini traveled north into Oregon from the California gold fields, foraging and living on wild duck eggs. When he returned to Italy he convinced many others including his son Rafael, to settle in Portland which he did in 1901.

The earliest account of a successful Italian businessman in Portland is that of Samuel N. Arrigoni who moved to Portland with his wife in 1856. He had been the chief officer aboard a steamship and in Portland opened a restaurant and later the Pioneer Hotel on the corner of Front and Washington streets. This was the oldest established hotel in Portland and the largest in the State

Samuel Arrigoni, the man from Milan, Italy moved to Astoria and helped to form the city's first fire department.

DeMartini and Arrigoni were among the vanguard of Italians.

The railroads ended Oregon's isolation had increased the foreign born population.

Abramo Cereghino, a Genoese, operated an Italian boarding house at 326 Front Street, Angiolo Alerto operated the Italian Hotel on the corner of Fifth and Pine. Campi's Hotel at 86th First Street was established and Vito Vitti started the Garibaldi grocery offering foods imported from Italy, as well as, a free labor agency, placing men at jobs on railroads, lumber and construction jobs throughout the Northwest.

Italians helped Italians, although wages paid to Italians were universally lower than those paid to other workers., Nevertheless these men took it, saved, settled with their families and played a constructive role in the development of Portland. Not the least of their contributions being artistic culture and cuisine.

"Italian Row" was located in East Portland on J Street, which is now Oak Street between First and Second, and the 'Italian Gardener's Garden' along the Willamette River at the foot of what is now Willamette Street. The first Italian colony in the city was set up on the edge of the Portland city dump on the present site of Duniway Park, south of S.W. Sheridan and West of S.W. Fourth Street.

Most Italians were situated between S.W. Clay and the west end of the present day Ross Island Bridge. A second and third Italian colony grew up in the Parkrose and Milwaukee areas. The next sizable Italian colony within the Portland city limits rose on the east side of the Willamette River in and around the present day Ladd's Addition. This colony became and remains the largest in the Portland area. It extends from the Willamette River east to S.E. 50th Avenue. The northern edge is Hawthorne Boulevard and the southern edge Powell.

Italians captured all phases of the fruit and

vegetable market and in 1901 the cornerstone of St. Michael's Church was laid at S.W. 4th and Mill. *The Italian Tribune* was founded in Seattle in 1889 and *La Stella* in Portland in 1910.

When Jason first moved to Portland he was invited to give his perspective of the legal ramifications of the Sacco-Vanzetti case.

This was so well received that he was befriended by two prominent Italian-American judges and a number of Italian-American attorneys who referred clients to him. He became aware of the early history of Italians in Portland and their rich cultural contribution. Perhaps for this reason he chose Italian neighborhoods and 'settlements' in which to meet his under-cover contact Susan as well as her Asian "friends."

Immediately upon arrival in Portland Jason sought out Greta.

Other than this fervent reunion Jason's return to Portland was uneventful and, with the help of Greta, he resumed working.

By this time the FBI had evaluated the documents Dieter had given to Jason. This material had been reviewed by experts in Washington and passed back to Jason suitably *sanitized* for transmission to Chinese agents. Misinformation was also incorporated into the material.

David Wong, the lead person at *Letni*, wanted to meet with Jason alone and Susan arranged a meeting to be held at the Viet Nam Memorial in Portland.

Yeah Chun who also worked with David wanted to attend but David would not allow it. He wanted to size up Jason for himself without the distraction of a woman being present. He also had questions about some of the information that was being passed back to him via Susan. It seems that Dieter had access to more than just the *Letni* research.

Jason was to pass along submarine tracking data and some material on missile tracking systems made available by Honeywell and Boeing to David. This material had been evaluated by FBI specialists in Washington and deemed reasonable to pass on as bait for the Chinese.

Indeed, David's 'control' in Beijing wanted more. The field of espionage that Dieter had been involved in seemed extensive and the Chinese believed he was serving multiple masters, including the Israeli and Indian governments. Pakistani monitoring of Indian government communications revealed an agent 'in place' in Portland.

Jason wanted to meet David at an Italian restaurant on the East Side but David wouldn't hear of it. The Viet Nam memorial it was to be.

On the appointed day, Jason parked his car in the lot and crossed the road to the Vietnam memorial, which consists of a concentric path encircling a 'punch bowl'. Six black granite semi-circular monuments line the walkway on the way to the top, the first commemorating the years 1959-65 and the next dated 1976. The final monument, at the top, is entitled MIA. The names on the granite are carved in white letters.

Five veterans and the parents of a marine killed in Vietnam began the project in 1982 and other veterans and volunteers contributed significantly. It is truly monument of, by and for the people.

Entering the park at the entrance below, Jason read the first introductory stone:

"The people of Oregon reconciled by sorrow and desiring to honor the dead, gave generously to this

gardens creation with the wish that all who come here may know refreshment and peace."

He then walked along one of two parallel paths leading to the Garden of Solace where a stone tablet announces the dedication: *"Dedicated to the 57,000 men and women of Oregon who served in Vietnam. 1959-1976."* Next to this, across from a circular fountain reads another inscription: *"So long as we are not forgotten we do not die. And thus this garden is a place of life."*

Jason walked the circular path, crossing a bridge over the parallel paths and fountain below. He came to the first black granite structure dated 1959 and began reading: *"While the war raged in Vietnam, day-to-day life in Oregon continued."* There was more, and in fact, each monument contained a mini-history of the time. He bided his time as instructed and walked to the 1968 structure. Looking over he spotted the park bench he was told to sit on. He was vaguely aware of a few women in the park walking their dogs and a maintenance person in the parking area.

There was little traffic to and from the Zoo nearby, otherwise the area was pristine. It started to rain and the clouds intensified the darkness of an already dismal day. He laughed to himself as he thought of the people of Portland making do with their weather system and playing golf in the rain, walking dogs and even sleeping out and having picnics.

Within a few minutes he was approached by a well-built Asian man wearing heavily rimmed eyeglasses that were clearly out of style. He was dressed in a dark business suit and white shirt. Black shoes and a dark necktie complimented his dress.

"So...you are Mr. Knox," he commented.

Jason wasn't sure if it was a question. "I'm Skip Knox."

Jason sensed that his adversary was confused with the use of a nickname and quickly added: "Jason Knox, attorney at law." He sounded very officious.

"My name is David, Mr. Knox. I am a friend of Susan's."

Jason did not need the introduction. The description was good enough. Paul had also shown him photos of David Wong. Besides, who else would be here on a rainy day wearing a business suit? For a moment he wondered how intelligent these intelligence people were but astutely took note of a sense of deviousness in his companion. More than deviousness it was a hardness he had seen before. An insensitivity. Here, next to him, sat a man who was purely utilitarian. An agent of the State.

"Please, I would like to know a little about you Mr. Knox."

This was a command not a request.

Jason had been briefed at Fort Worden and later by Susan, on how to address his answers. His answers worked like a charm.

David relaxed focusing his questions on Jason's personal life. Had he ever been married? Did he have any children? Were his parents living? What kind of work did his father do? What were his interests in school? Did he serve in the Army?

After about 15 minutes of this Jason attempted to turn their meeting into a conversation. He knew he would not really learn anything about David, but he wanted to soften tone of what was transpiring. This was indeed helpful as David responded to Jason's queries without hesitation. He would almost immediately bring the subject back to Jason. This was to be no idle chitchat session.

Their meeting lasted over an hour and fifteen minutes and at the conclusion David asked if Jason had a present for him, at which point Jason handed over a newspaper that was wrapped around a heavy brown envelope.

David took the paper. "Thank you Mr. Knox. Goodbye. See you again I'm sure."

Jason nodded agreement and waited about ten minutes, waiting for David to drive away, reading the remainder of his newspaper before leaving.

As he walked down toward the parking lot he became aware of someone off in the distance waving his arms. After considering this situation he continued toward his car, thinking it best to get out of there.

Sensing danger, he walked deliberately and alertly.

Nearby a brown dog was running in a circle building up speed. Jason took notice and continued on his path.

Suddenly the dog began running, turned sideways and hurled himself at Jason's back, knocking him to the ground.

Jason felt the hard thump and fell face forward into the wet grass and mud. He was momentarily stunned and looking up met the eyes of a very angry dog. The animal's eyes were slanted, ears were back and face was distorted. Its muzzle reminded him of a bear. A growling sound from deep inside this animal caused Jason to remain motionless. He was eye to eye with an animal that, so it seemed to him, wanted to eat him alive. The dog's mouth was open and he could see its black tongue.

Jason didn't know what to think but he sure as hell wasn't going to make any quick moves. It had all happened so fast! What to do now? The blast took him by surprise.

He and the dog were both startled when the explosion occurred.

Regaining his senses Jason realized that his car and a white van next to it had been blown to pieces. Someone had tried to kill him, or so it seemed.

In less than a minute a man dressed in jeans and a rain jacket was standing next to him offering a hand.

Once on his feet Jason realized the dog was sitting quietly and watching his every move. He wasn't going anyplace.

The man who helped him up was vaguely familiar but Jason couldn't place him. He was still shaken. "Er...thanks. What the hell has happened?"

"You're welcome Skip. I'll explain later."

Somewhat taken back Jason asked: "What? Do I know you?" He began to surmise that this man was more than just a passer by or park stroller.

"I'm Special Agent Berger. We met at Fort Worden."

"Oh...yeah...I remember now."

"Good," responded Berger..."Now lets get out of here and I will tell you what I know, which isn't much."

They headed toward an upward path.

Jason kept his eye on the dog that followed close behind.

Once behind the Forestry Building two more agents met them, one of who looked like a maintenance worker. A car was waiting nearby.

When he realized the dog was going to sit on the back seat, Jason elected to ride in front with the driver. Agents Berger and Stayton sat in back, the Chow between them.

"Will somebody tell me what just the hell happened?" Jason raised his voice for the occasion. "And where did this dog come from? I thought he wanted to eat me up."

'Book saved you life Skip."

131

By now Jason was even more agitated. "Who the fuck is Book?"

The Agents could tell he was frightened and just beginning to comprehend his brush with death. They understood how he felt.

Agent Berger responded in a very soft voice: "Book is my Chow Chow. I picked this breed because it doesn't arouse suspicions of being a police dog like a German Shepard might. This breed is tough, and although difficult to train, very reliable. The Beaverton Police Department has one of the best dog trainer-handlers in the Northwest. A policewoman named Lori Buell. She helped us with the special needs training for Book. We capitalized on a few thousand years of genetic imprinting as well as the dog's loyalty.

"What?" responded Jason, somewhat calmed down by now. "What the hell are you talking about?"

Berger wanted to distract his companion from what had just happened. He well understood the value of gab in a situation like this. "Well...that behavior you just saw. That's how these Chow Chows fought the bears in Tibet. They build up speed and knock their pray down. Then they go for the throat or ankles."

Jason turned to face Berger more directly, eyes wide open, pupils clearly dilated.

"Oh don't worry, he would only have bit you once, if that. These dogs don't maul people unless they are themselves in danger. He's trained. One bite and he backs off. And then he'll wait."

"Yeah, but what if he bit my throat or face?"

"It's more likely he would have gone for your ankles to keep you down. At least that's how we trained him. Back of the necks a possibility too."

The Agent realized he might be frightening Jason but wanted to keep the conversation off the event-the explosion.

Jason was beginning to formulate the idea that a bomb had been planted in his car.

Berger went on talking about how Chow Chow's originated in Tibet and were used by the Chinese to protect the royal nurseries and the concubines as well. He spoke about how the Chinese fought their removal from Chinese soil feeding them rubber bands so they would die on shipboard. "The Chow Chow is at least 3000 years old, probably originally from the Arctic Circle and then migrating to Mongolia and Siberia. Some believe the Chow Chow came about through a crossing of the old Mastiff of Tibet and the Samoyed from Northern Siberia. Others believe the Chow was the original ancestor of the Samoyed and a number of other breeds."

Berger certainly knew something about dogs.

"Likely the Chow was a distinct breed in China as early as and maybe earlier than 1000 B.C. The chow is an outdoor dog of great stamina. It can hunt; pull a sled and herd cattle and sheep. It certainly herded you Skip."

Jason flashed a sardonic smile.

Berger went on to discuss the origin of the word Chow derived from slang Chinese meaning edible.

There was more about eating dogs than Jason wanted to hear about.

Queen Victoria was given a Chow Chow in 1865 but it was in 1880 that the Chow entered the history of England in the personage of Chinese Puzzle, a black Chow bitch who was exhibited at the Crystal Palace show in London.

Jason understandably didn't want to hear any more. "Let's get back to what happened!" he demanded.

Berger explained that a car bomb had been planted in Jason's car.

"But why would the Chinese want to kill me for Christ's sake, I just met with one of their agents? I know they want more information. Killing me would stop the conduit."

"Maybe," replied Berger. "Maybe they think someone else would take over. Maybe someone more reliable than you. Maybe David didn't trust you. Then again, maybe not. Maybe this was a mistake."

"Oh hell...a mistake?! It seems to me that bomb had to be planted before David made up his mind about me. Am I right?"

There was no response.

"Well, isn't that logical? Am I right?"

The agent next to Berger spoke up: "We're not sure Mr. Knox. We can't fit all the pieces together yet. But we will. We will. Give it some time."

"In the meantime who else is going to try to blow me up?" responded Jason. He was clearly asking for some guidance.

He was beginning to wonder why the hell he let himself get mixed up in all of this. This was the second time his life was put in jeopardy. Three strikes and your out. He was not a cat with nine lives. With this thought he turned to the dog being careful to keep his hands to himself.

"Where did that dog get the name Book?"

Berger explained that he was from Pennsylvania. A Penn State grad. He liked the movie *Witness* which was filmed in Pennsylvania Dutch Country. The detective in the movie was played by Harrison Ford. His name was Book. This information struck Jason like a ton of bricks. Greta was from Pennsylvania. From Lancaster County. Pennsylvania Dutch country.

Was there a connection? Was she somehow involved in all of this directly? Why was she staying around to work anyway? He started to ask Berger what he knew about Greta but thought better of it. Besides this agent wasn't going to give him any information about anybody. That had become clear.

At least he could talk with Paul. And where was Paul anyway? Jason had one important question he insisted on asking.

As they pulled up alongside of his condominium, he turned to the agents. "By the way, how did you know enough to stop me? How did you find out the car was set to blow?"

Berger broke out in a broad grin. "Annuit Coeptis!"

"A new what," asked Jason, clearly irritated at this response.

"Oh...some of us older Agents have a motto in the Bureau. Annuit Coeptis. We don't discuss it much outside the Bureau.

You can find the motto on the reverse Great Seal of the United States. It literally means that God has favored our undertakings."

"You mean it was luck?" replied Jason.

"Well...in a way," replied Berger. "It really means more than that. In a sense, We with a capital "W" are favoring your undertakings. We are watching over all. God sees all. We see all."

Jason had had enough. He wasn't going to get anything out of this double talk. This stuff was bordering on megalomania. What's worse Berger believed in this hocus-pocus. And what's even worse...his life was in the hands of these guys. At least the dog knew what he was doing!!

Greta was waiting for Jason when he arrived. She already knew what had happened. Paul called and asked if she would keep an eye on Jason and let him know if he had a problem or needed help in any way. Greta had readily agreed. She was worried. Very worried. This wasn't supposed to happen.

As soon as he saw Greta, Jason threw his arms around her and began furiously kissing her. His hand moved to her crotch area and he began massaging her through her dress. When death is on the doorstep, love becomes paramount.

God had given you one face, and you make yourselves another.

Shakespeare
Hamlet III,1

ELEVEN

YEAH CHUN

Jason held Greta all night long. He did not want to let go of her. She in turn nurtured him.

Jason's dreams were troubling. In one dream fragment he was trying to rescue two children who were being engulfed by a tidal wave. It was obvious that he, along with the children would be submerged. In another he visualized himself in a casket at his own funeral. He was not really dead but was afraid to open his eyes. Was he merely playing possum? Or was he really dead?

At breakfast the following morning he spoke little, certainly wishing to avoid discussing the dream material he had become so sensitized to.

During stressful times he would experience a re-emergence of posttraumatic symptoms and his dreams would mesh with childhood experiences and take on an entirely new direction. Through therapy and study he had learned to decipher the secret hidden language of dreams and this helped him master the anxiety that threatened his integrity.

After breakfast Greta decided to go to the office and Jason elected to stay at the condo. Dressed in blue jeans and "T-shirt" he lounged back in his easy chair and sipped coffee.

Thus caught up in his reveries the bell chimed. Peering through the visor it took him a few moments to fully register the image before him.

Slowing opening the door he blurted out: "Oh God! What do you want?"

"Good morning Mr. Knox. Mr. Jason Knox, attorney at law, doctor of jurisprudence." It was a flat direct and not unfriendly statement.

Jason's response was less charitable: "I didn't know you could pronounce big words like that."

"May I come in?"

"You might as well, you're here. What is it this time?" He motioned detective Alexander to a chair and sat back in his recliner.

"I'm here to sell you some stock in the Portland Police Bureau Mr. Knox. I mean, being that you are one of our best customers and all you might as well own a piece of the rock." Alexander was in a playful mood.

Jason waited. All of these cop types seemed to have a weird sense of humor. And they liked puzzling statements. It gave them some sense of control, or so Jason thought. He was in no mood for jokes or puzzles.

"I saw the incident report on your car. You know, don't you that someone tried to kill you? Explosions like this are no accident especially when they happen to you. You're in the fast lane. High visibility and high action. What arrrree you up to?"

"Detective I haven't filed a complaint. There's no suspect and I'm tired. And what business is it of yours?" Jason was taking out all of his hostility on the detective who was simply trying to do his job.

"Well, first of all it's my job to investigate attempted homicides. Secondly, this is my street corner Mr. Knox. This is my city and I care about what happens. You may live through this but some dumb schmuck may get himself killed because you're not in favor with the Valentine card company. Just think of it this way, Jason, I answer to a higher power." Alexander was trying to soften the conversation.

"Yes," Jason responded, "your ego."

Jason observed the deep red flush moving up from the detective's neck into his face. The vessels stood out in his neck causing his collar to appear tight. Very tight. He regretted the comment but it was too late.

Alexander stood up and walked to the door, slamming it as he left.

Jason sat down in his recliner, head in hands, trying to make sense out of what had happened to him. His confusion only deepened when he recalled the dream fragments from the night before. To make matters worse, Greta suspected him of having an affair with Susan. Whenever he wasn't in the office he was meeting with Susan, or so it seemed to Greta. Susan also telephoned frequently and Jason closed the door when her calls came in. The tension in his relationship with Greta had manifested itself in quieter lunches and dinners and what seemed to be a distancing curiosity evident in Greta's demeanor. Deciding to turn off his thoughts he turned on the T.V. and zoned out for most of the day. After a quiet evening alone, a sandwich and a few glasses of wine he called it quits and slept through the night.

The morning *Oregonian* detailed how the third body of a young woman had been found in Forest Park. Police suspected a serial killer was on the loose. It was of some slight consolation that he realized that some people in town had bigger problems than he did. On impulse he went to his refrigerator and discarded any food that was not sealed or in cans. He discarded the open can of peanuts and an opened package of crackers. Jason worried about being poisoned by someone and he was becoming obsessional in his behavior. The serial killer article had precipitated more anxiety.

He left for the office.

Later in the day Jason met with Susan at Demarco's restaurant in the Italian section. He sipped wine while she had a cup of tea. Susan had no explanation for the bombing incident. She believed the meeting with David had gone off well and now Yeah Chun, her co-worker, wanted to meet him. She chose the Zoo area for the meeting, not far from the Vietnam Memorial.

"Oh great. Is this going to be another bombing?"

"Ohhhh. No. Don't worry. We can watch you carefully on the Zoo grounds. And this time take the Max to Washington Station. Take the elevator up to ground level and this will place you at Les Aucoin Center. Walk a few yards across to the Zoo. And, Oh, that reminds me, this is for you." Susan handed Jason a newspaper. "Page D-3 has a parcel attached. It is enough money to buy another car. The exact amount to replace your other one. Any questions?"

"Yes...are you into annuit coeptis too?"

"Well...you've been talking to Berger. That's his thing. Those old guys just don't give up. He's a Georgia cracker. Just take him in stride. The FCI brings in all kinds of people."

"FCI?"

"Yes, that's Foreign Counter Intelligence. It's what we in the Bureau call this business."

"Oh."

"Yeah is a friend of Liu Baiyu, Ou Yang Shanzun, Chin Zhaoyie and Wang Yang."

"Do I know these guys," replied Jason. "Or should I?"

"These four men crossed North China with Evans Carlson about 60 years ago. She also knows Yao Wei who was a fellow at the Woodrow Wilson International Center for Scholars, Harvard and Stanford Universities. He has been involved with the China International Trust and Investment Corporation and has served as Chairman of the Board for Citifor. What this means is that Yeah moves in high circles and is well thought of by many in power. In some respects she's a sleeper. She is also a member of the "inner sanctum" and the Friends of Evans Carlson group. Zhao Zhen and Zheng Guox with the Chinese Counsel in San Francisco have been apprised of the contacts with you. What this all means is that things are heating up. His Excellency Liang Yufan Ambassador and former Deputy Permanent representative of the People's Republic of China to the United Nations has been made aware of the economic consequences of your role in this situation and suddenly, Mr. Knox, you have become the focus of much attention. Much indeed. In the eyes of some Chinese you have become very important."

Jason didn't know whether to laugh or cry. He knew a little about Rewi Alley, Agnes Smedley, Edgar Snow and Dr. Ma Haide, but these names, with the exception of Carlson and Stilwell, were new to him. Paul had briefed him on Han Xu who was China's representative to the U.S. and had especially strong statements to make about the Taiwan issue, citing the Shanghai Communiqué of 1972 as the cornerstone of China's perspective of U.S. unfulfilled policy. He wondered where all of this fit in with him and what it might have to do with being attacked and then nearly being blown up. Nevertheless, he listened quietly as

Susan spoke.

Soon his mind drifted to thoughts of Greta.

Somehow all of his fantasies at this point intermingled with the ideas of Felix Frankfurter. These legal-philosophical ideas were a source of surcease for him.

Susan observed that Jason was growing weary and another meeting was arranged for one week later.

Portland, in addition to being known as the City of Roses, is also known as The City of Bridges. Depending on which ones you count there are between 7 and 9 bridges scanning the Willamette and Columbia Rivers. Jason drove over the Steel Bridge to meet Susan at the appointed time at Cafe Lena's, a trendy restaurant that caters to writers and poets. He waited and waited, ordered a light lunch and waited some more. No Susan.

He finished his lunch and left.

Late that afternoon he received a telephone call from Susan.

"What happened? Where were you?"

"I had a slight accident...some chemicals spilled. A conduit burst exactly where I stood. I spent the better part of the afternoon in a cold shower."

"Are you all right?"

"Yes...minus a little pride. I don't like taking my clothes off in front of a bunch of gawking men."

"Well, keep your clothes on next time." replied Jason. He was trying to make light of the situation.

Suddenly he became aware that his office door was open and Greta, no doubt, could hear the conversation.

"The security people here said it was industrial sabotage," replied Susan, not responding to the humor.

"Oh...I see," replied Jason, trying to speak in a

muffled voice. "When do we meet again?"

Susan responded after a lengthy pause, "On Thursday visit the Zoo at around 1 PM. Take your camera and take pictures of the animals. Wander over to the African section and then casually walk over to the wolf habitat. You will meet my co-worker there. There's no need for us to meet now. That's it."

"That's it?" replied Jason.

"That's it," replied Susan as she hung up.

It seemed to Jason that she was abrupt, but then again when he thought about it she could have been seriously burned or even killed with the toxic exposure.

After exiting the Max elevator at surface level, Jason spotted a uniformed transit security guard, whom he thought, or at least hoped, was an FBI agent in disguise. He crossed from Aucoin Plaza to the Zoo entrance, purchased a ticket and then casually began walking and photographing the goats and tigers along the way. He almost forgot the purpose of his visit since, at the designated position, photographing the wolves in natural habitat was a special treat for him. He had once dreamed of being a wildlife photographer and had even used this guise as 'cover' once. He knew how to handle cameras and the FBI capitalized on his skill.

"Beautiful, aren't they?" The middle aged Asian woman next to him was wearing a gray-brownish understated business suit, not at all out of place in this setting. At first glance she appeared a visitor, perhaps from San Francisco. To Jason she was the quintessence of understatement. No jewelry or adornments and her hair was close cropped outlining her high cheekbones and slender face. All in all she gave the appearance of a successful businesswoman relaxing and sightseeing.

Before Jason could respond she added, "Perhaps

you might help me with my camera Mr. Knox. I seem to be having a little trouble."

After a slight pause, Jason sized up the situation. He noticed the impeccable English accent and oddly remembered a comment that Henry Kissinger had made about Chou En Lai. His English was so good that one day, when they were walking, he stumbled and his expression was American slang rather than Chinese. He was thinking in English!

Jason helped Yeah Chun with her camera. She did not introduce herself. They walked and talked. Yeah Chun asked questions and Jason answered, doing most of the talking. Unlike the meeting with David, her questions were technical and not personal. This would be very helpful to the Feds in Washington as these questions provided pieces of the puzzle that were missing. This included information regarding what the Chinese already knew and what they needed to know. Misinformation could then be provided.

Yeah Chun proved a sophisticated university trained woman. She was clearly very intelligent and dedicated, both to her work and to China. There was also personal warmth in her style and this seemed to Jason to be genuine. She provided Jason with an interesting piece of information in acknowledging awareness that the FBI had planted listening devices in the new Chinese consulate building in San Francisco, during its construction.

All in all Jason felt he had made a good impression on Yeah Chun and he had certainly come away with some useful information. His sense of China and the Chinese Secret Service was coalescing. He felt more comfortable and at least thought he could handle what might come up. He also realized he was being groomed to meet Chinese government officials but it was clear he would have to provide technical answers to the questions Yeah Chun asked and then some. But this was not his problem. He would either be given this information or disinformation or the operation would be off.

Things were happening fast. The FBI tradition seemed to be to tell Jason nothing or very little about the operation itself but the information he passed seemed to be satisfying his customers.

But some things were not fitting into place and no one was giving him the answers. The missing pieces of the puzzle. He thought about all of this on the way home. It seemed to start with Dieter. Or did it start with the arrival of Greta? Dieter's death, the envelopes, the attack on him, the ransacking of the apartment, the training in Port Townsend and Whidbey, the secret meetings, the bombing, the Chinese agents? His falling in love?
He had learned to look for patterns but could find none. Some things seemed straightforward enough but there was too much ambiguity. He sensed something out of joint. What was worse, he didn't know what to do about it. Jason walked from the Max station to his condo. Rain was coming down in buckets and he was soaked and cold when he arrived. Finding the note from Greta didn't help matters any. He sensed what it might say:
"Dear Jason,

I think it best that I take a leave of absence from work. I'll be in Central Oregon   visiting my parents for an indefinite time. Have made arrangements for a temp to cover the office. Don't worry, all the briefs are typed and I went over the schedule with Mildred who will be in tomorrow. I also left her my number if she has any questions.

Take care, Greta.

This was right to the quick of things. Matter of fact. No Love Greta, just Greta.

Jason thought better of calling her. She was not the type of person one pushed. She had that stoic determined central Pennsylvania personality.

Jason had seen better days and there was no indication on the horizon that things would improve, either in his personal life or with the intrigues he was caught up in. Now he had to face this situation alone.

He was aware of the impending visit of the Chinese Ambassador and a number of so-called dignitaries, not a few of who were intelligence agents. How this visit would effect him was not certain. He wasn't even sure the Chinese trusted him and he knew enough about the psychology of recruiting agents to know that their mistrust would be reasonable. Still, they didn't seem to know much about his past. Or did they? He recalled that the Chinese liked George Bush and were happy when he was elected President, even though he had been head of the CIA. They were capable of overlooking some things. Perhaps accepting was a better word. Thousands of years of a rich culture, the Civilization that gave us gunpowder, had much to teach about tolerance.

As a source of comfort, Jason thought of Greta and wondered if their relationship would ever be viable. He fell asleep thinking of the time they had had sex in the office standing against the wall. Through this memory he tried to keep her alive for the moment, repressing the thought that she had left.

The great king of kings
Hath in the tables of his law commanded
That thou shalt do no murder.

Shakespeare
Richard III I,4

TWELVE

GUNTER

Gunter Hauschke, a nondescript man lived with his wife Helga in a nondescript house in a lower middle class neighborhood in Southeast Portland. Of German descent from Wisconsin, he was one of these nameless, yet faithful, workers who keep the city functioning. He, and people like him, brought to reality the Portland City motto inscribed in all official vehicles: 'a city that works'.

His wife Helga can best be described as chubby, loving, a good cook and a woman with a harsh sounding giggle. It was the giggle that Gunter loved. He was a devoted husband and she a devoted wife. They had no children nor wanted any. 'The Mrs', as Gunter referred to Helga, had a small white dog of mixed extraction. She saw to it that both the dog and Gunter had plenty to eat. Behind their home they had a small yard where Helga planted flowers.

The Hauschke's had few friends but were well thought of by their neighbors. Gunter liked his beer and sausage and Helga her Poochie. On Saturdays they liked to go mushroom hunting, something Helga had been taught by her German grandmother who survived the war in Europe by finding and hoarding mushrooms. On

Sunday they breakfasted late, sat around reading *The Oregonian* and walked in the park. Their vacations were spent at Cannon Beach. Gunter had been recruited for his job and they moved to Portland in the mid 80's. They were content. Gunter preferred working the evening shift and sleeping late in the morning. Helga also had time to herself this way and she liked the late night TV talk shows, especially those that made her giggle.

One such evening he kissed Helga goodbye, grabbed his lunchbox and thermos of heavily sugared coffee and left for work.

She was never to see him again. She would never be told the circumstances of his death.

*The ultimate measure of a man is not where he stands
In moments of comfort and convenience, but where he
Stands at times of challenge and controversy.*

Martin Luther King, Jr.

*Mine honour is my life; both grow in one;
Take honour from me, and my life is done.*

**Shakespeare
Richard II, II,1**

THIRTEEN

WALK EAST ON BURNSIDE

Paul arrived at the Portland FBI office early. He peered into the security device that instantly 'photographed' his retina for identity recognition, walked over to his desk and read the dispatch he had been called about.

GSG9 of German Intelligence had forwarded information of multiple intelligence penetrations in the communications and high tech industry in the area. He scanned the material and realized this complicated matters with the Chinese operation.

Jason, of course, knew none of this when he awoke.

The weather was heavily overcast and a sense of darkness pervaded his living quarters. In the bathroom he noticed some of Susan's cosmetics and recalled that Greta had probably seen them. She was a class act though and never mentioned her increasing jealousy of Susan. Kiss-kiss, bang bang thought Jason.

Shortly before leaving for the office to meet Mildred, he received a call from Susan. Speaking of the devil, he thought.

There was to be a planning meeting. Paul, Susan and some unnamed agents would be present. "Is 1 o'clock today O.K.?" asked Susan. "Is your schedule tight? We can work around your schedule if need be, but we need to meet in a day or two."

"One is fine," responded Jason. "Where?"

"Drive south on 99W. A little way outside of Dundee turn right at the Lafayette exit. Make a left on the main street and then a right at Bill's Market. Follow the road up the hill and turn in at the Trappist Abbey. The parking lot is on the right below the Abbey. It will be very quiet there and very very private. We will have a vantage point if any unexpected visitors show up."

"All the way out there? responded Jason."

"Yes," replied Susan as she hung up.

Even in the rain the drive was beautiful and Jason was overcome with an enormous sense of peace as he approached the administration buildings and Church at the Abbey. The parking lot was easy to find and he secluded himself on the lower level.

The four of them met in an unmarked car. One agent stood outside. Paul did most of the talking.

"Tomorrow night you will meet the big tomato. Susan has all the data you'll need. Start out at around 8 PM and park downtown. Use a lot if you have to. Then walk east on Burnside. A Chinese agent will meet you at the China Gate. No doubt you've seen this large ornate structure with the dragons."

Jason had passed it many times but never really stopped in this area. It was a seedy part of town and he avoided it.

"There is an adult book store just behind the

columns. Don't go in. Don't go into Chinatown. Repeat, do NOT go into Chinatown. You can conduct your business behind the columns. Hand over the briefcase and be done with it as quickly as possible. Your adversary may have a few questions but keep it short. We will triangulate you. Your code identification will be "Nesika Klatawa Sahale," so memorize it."

"What's that asked Jason?"

"Susan picked it. It's the motto of a local climbing club. The Mazamas. The Chinese agreed. Their response will be in English: 'We climb ever higher.' When you hear this hand over the briefcase. Susan will fill you in on the details. She'll be behind you, walking east on Burnside. About a half mile behind. You'll both be wired. Questions?"

"Yes, how much do I respond to? And what about the triangulation?"

"Use your judgment on the questions. The triangulation will be typical. We'll attach a homing device to you and three of our agents will monitor and pass on the information to our command van. I'll be in the van on the east side of Burnside over the bridge. Susan will be behind you. One of our agents will be in Chinatown and one in downtown Portland. You'll have plenty of cover. You'll also wear a carapace."

"Carapace?"

"Yes, a protective shield, at least on your torso. We'll need open areas for the honing and monitoring devices."

Jason thought, "just like the Feds". Why didn't he just say bulletproof vest?

Susan continued the briefing. Finally she said, "Whatever you do, don't lose the wire or the honing device. I'll also monitor you. I'll move in at any sign of trouble. Their people want to meet you and check both your information and reliability."

"Why can't we meet someplace else? Like a restaurant or hotel room?" queried Jason.

"The reasons are complicated. The Chinese want to meet on or near their own turf and the entrance to Chinatown is convenient for them. They can retreat into one of the Tongs if things go awry. Also the operatives who are here with the diplomatic corps realize they are less likely to be under surveillance in this location. There is also less chance of being monitored. Also, whatever you do stay out of the adult bookstore. We don't want you lured into a situation behind closed doors."

"I get the impression this is a big deal but I don't fully understand why," responded Jason.

Susan was obdurate in her response. "This is the story and this is how it will go down. Getting cold feet Mr. Knox?"

"No, not really. I'm ready," replied Jason.

Jason dolefully drove home. He was alone and facing the unknown. It was too late to back out now. Even if he did he wasn't sure what he was backing away from. He arrived back at his condo around six, prepared an omelet for dinner and sat alone for a few hours. In spite of the downpour Jason went out for a walk. He was restless and needed to get out. He was girding for an encounter and didn't know what to expect or how to judge his adversary.

That night he dreamt he was on a Civil War battlefield at Army Headquarters. President Lincoln and General Meade were conferring and Jason was trying to understand the battle strategy. Lincoln appeared doleful. Meade dour. As Jason experienced a fitful sleep the rain pour outside continued. It rained and rained and rained and rained.

Mildred was a delightful woman who had the office situation well in control. She was a late middle-aged grandmother who returned to the workforce partly to find something to do and partly for financial reasons. Jason was comfortable with her and with her seeming ability to help with his law practice. Even in picking a replacement, Greta had chosen well.

Jason could not concentrate on work and after a light lunch at The University Club, with one of the local judges, he walked over to the Art Museum and spent a few hours. The rain had subsided by this time but it was still dark, damp and gloomy.

Jason drove to the medical complex and parked in an area that allowed a broad visage of the city. This was 'The Hill' and he could be alone there.

He tried to visualize where he would be later that night and imagined himself an elf amidst the jungle. He thought about the Abbey he had been at the day before and the dichotomy of his existence. It was more than just peaceful there. It was the absence of malice that struck him the most. A vacuum where love rushes in. He remembered the dream of the night before and one of Lincoln's sayings: *"If a man doesn't shine his own boots, whose boots does he shine."*

In a Zen sense, Jason was shining his own boots. He was doing something he needed to do. Deep down inside he had to respond to his sense of honor. He was not one to walk away from duty and wondered where all of this would lead.

Jason, Susan and Paul met in a room next to the basement morgue at St. Vincent's Hospital. This was both a convenient and private place to be. No windows, no intrusion and no problems. Jason was wired and handed the briefcase.

"Don't open it," commented Paul. "Just carry it and hand it over when you hear the code words...and.don't let it out of your sight in the meantime."

Jason was silent. He had little to say and watched with amusement as the FBI technician plied his craft. He wanted to avoid being captious at this very critical point in time.

They individually filed out of the room and the hospital to their respective vehicles. Jason wondered when he would see Paul and Susan again.

He went home and opened a can of tuna for dinner. Luckily he had showered earlier in the day. He checked his monitoring devices, secured his vest picked up the briefcase and left his condo.

He found a place to park off of Burnside behind Powell's Bookstore.

Susan was to take up position at 7:50 as Jason began his sojourn. It was not raining but the heavy over-cast had brought on darkness a little sooner than usual. Jason did take some unaccustomed comfort in this as un-warranted as it might be.

Jason heard static and above the static Susan's voice. "Jason, go back to your car."

"Why? What's the problem?"

"We are three hours too early," responded Susan. "The Chinese have changed the time. I assume as a security precaution. I tried to reach you earlier but couldn't get through your phone lines. We hadn't yet set up this monitor. Go back and return at 10:45. Kill a few hours."

"Will do," responded Jason.

He thought of stopping in at Mary's Club, a local strip bar. Under the circumstances this seemed appropriate but he opted for the safer circumstance, the bar at the Benson Hotel.

Jason sipped club sodas and read the paper in the comfortable lounging area. He tried to look inconspicuous and hoped he wouldn't run into any of his friends. This might cause a delay and create some awkwardness . He wondered if something hadn't gone wrong already.

After what seemed an interminable delay he started out again, taking up position on Burnside. Radio communications were resumed and Jason was confident that Susan was in place behind him. Traffic was slight and aside from an occasional derelict the streets were empty.

As instructed, Jason walked slowly, measuring his steps and biding his time. His only concern was the intermittent loss of his radio communication. This was either a malfunction or a jamming device was being used.

Fifteen minutes into the walk Paul radioed Susan to abort the operation. "Abort. Abort. That's an order!"

Jason did not receive the message or if he did, he did not acknowledge it. He kept walking.

Although the Feds were assured there would be no ship traffic that evening, something had gone wrong and the bridge was going up. There would be no way for Paul and the agents to reach Jason if something went wrong.

Little did Paul, or anyone for that matter; know that Gunter Hauschke, the bridge tender, was lying on the floor with a 9mm bullet in his head. He was stone dead and the bridge was up.

Susan did receive the message but out of concern for Jason she began running to catch up to him. To her, aborting the operation meant saving her partner in the process.

It was as if a shadow leaped out from a doorway and before she knew it she had been tripped. She thrust her hands forward to break the fall. Quickly pushing herself up she was face to face with her assailant who thrust a knife into her side. Pulling it out rapidly he slashed her forearm as she had raised it to defend herself.

Susan did not, however, fit the victim profile. This was no dress rehearsal. By training and instinct she knew she had minutes perhaps moments to act before blood loss might render her unconscious.

In an instant the teachings of Miyamoto Musashi and *A Book Of Five Rings* coincided with her Academy training. She had come to life. Two ancient cultures merged in the penultimate expression of her survival. She was fighting for her life. The kick to his groin brought her assailant forward and this was followed by a reverse kick to his jaw. He fell backwards, twisting to the left and Susan landed another kick to his right temple. She hoped to fracture what she knew to be a delicate artery in that area. Now *he* was a victim, and she landed her fourth kick at the base of his head. She heard the sound of bone cracking and turned to run for help. She knew *he* would not be following but wasn't sure who else was around.

"Officer down. Need assistance," she fitfully radioed as she ran down West on Burnside. She was running to save her life.

Reaching Broadway, Susan ran in front of an approaching cab. "Help. Take me to the hospital...I'm bleeding to death."

"I don't want no trouble lady," responded the cabbie that didn't want to get in the middle of a domestic dispute.

Susan was able to reach her blood soaked credentials, which she flashed.

Although barely able to see them the cabbie listened: "FBI. I'm bleeding to death. Get me to a hospital. I'm Special Agent Susan..."

The cab driver was outside by this time and literally poured her into the back seat of his cab. He wondered who would pay for the upholstery damages but didn't want trouble with the FBI. Besides, there was a hint of the Good Samaritan in him.

He drove like a bat out of hell and was thinking what a story he'd have to tell his wife. Maybe someone would even think he was a hero.

At the Emergency Room entrance he pressed continuously on the horn, jumped out and began dragging Susan into the hospital. "I got an FBI lady whose bleedin' to death! Hurry up! Help!"

Almost simultaneously, at the other end of town, Jason had his share of problems as well. They were soon to reach a critical point. Paul and his agents were unable to get across the Burnside Bridge and so had gone northward hoping to bypass Burnside and come in from the Broadway Bridge. They had no way of knowing that this bridge was blocked as well, this time with a large semi that had jackknifed.

Jason reached the imposing columns of The China Gate.

His communication system was, by this time, completely jammed and he had no idea of Susan's plight.

He hesitated a moment before going into the shadows of the columns, remembering not to traverse too far into Chinatown. He also kept away from the side door of the Adult Bookstore.

A man stepped forward and as Jason uttered the code words he heard the first shot. The small arms fire hit his Kevlar vest knocking him against the wall. He struggled for breath and to stay on his feet. His chest hurt as well. He had no way of knowing that his contact person was lying in a hotel room close by with his throat cut and David was lying outside his apartment, the apparent victim of a suicide.

The next shot shattered Jason's arm. As he passed out, he barely heard the third resounding crack. His lights went out. It was all over.

O tiger's heart wrapped in a woman's hide!

3 Henry VI, I 4

FOURTEEN

HELEN

Helen's seniority allowed her to be assigned to the 4:PM - 12:AM shift, known as the third watch or afternoon relief, depending on longevity with the Portland Police Bureau. Older 911 employees remembered the shift as the third watch changed, in name, a few years ago to the afternoon relief. Although classified as a civilian employee titled 'emergency dispatcher', Helen knew police work through a vicarious education as one of the communications lifelines of the police bureau. While she had not seen it all from the windowless confines of the radio room, in her twenty-four years, she had heard it all over the police frequencies including, more than once, the words of a dying police officer calling for help a final time.

Helen was viewed, by her 15 co-workers, as a veteran dispatcher who was cool as ice under the stress of emergencies. She had learned to conceal the nagging fear that a mistake by her could cost the life of a police officer. Sending help to the wrong address, missing a radio call or failing to recognize trouble, that was not readily apparent, gnawed at her sense of responsibility in ways only an emergency police dispatcher could know or appreciate.

Helen had what can only be described as an infectious smile and an elegant beauty that only comes with age and wisdom and radiates to everyone lucky enough to be around.

She was visited frequently by officers who brought her little gifts, boxes of candy and flowers in appreciation for her skills in emergencies.

Her personnel file was decorated with departmental commendations for coolness under fire. The cops knew her voice on the radio and she knew theirs. Her voice meant that the street officer was being looked after by a pro that had demonstrated the ability to make the right decisions under extreme stress. They knew Helen would not leave them hanging. They did not know of her inner fear of not holding up her end-a fear that was to be sorely tested in about sixty seconds.

She had just returned from break and resumed her place at the circular console, carefully placing the headphones to avoid messing up her recently styled hairdo. She thought it would probably be a boring night. The entire week had been quiet and Helen even thought of taking a book to work but this was against regulations. She sat daydreaming about her weekend plans when suddenly the computer screen in front came alive and the calls became frantic...she quickly grasped that something in the City of Roses had gone awry. That something was becoming unbelievable even for a seasoned police dispatcher.

At the adjacent console, Helen's co-worker, Carole, was taking a call from Woodland Park Hospital on the East side. A city employee was in the emergency room, the apparent victim of a gunshot wound. His condition was undetermined. Helen took calls originating on the West side. She went into what she called 'combat mode'. Something inexplicable was happening...

"Unit 476-Code 4. Officer down...Broadway and...Correction...Good Samaritan Hospital. Officer down. Unit 519-homicide! Request secure area. Apartment house at 641 Couch. Asian male, approximately 45. Throat slashed. Second Asian male three blocks south. Apparent suicide-possible homicide. Possible related. Unit 518 double shooting - possible homicide. Asian Gate-entrance to Chinatown. Backup requested for all units. Repeat backup for all units."

When your vile daggers
Hack'd one another in the sides of Caesar,
You show'd your teeth like apes.

Shakespeare
Julius Caesar V,1

We that are true lovers run into strange capers.

Shakespeare
As You Like It, II,4

FIFTEEN

BARNES

Jason's eyes opened slowly. At first his mind did not register what he was looking at, as the Teddy Bear came into perspective. A nursing assistant was rearranging his bed linen and checking to se that the IV flow was continuous.

"Where am I? What happened?"

"You're in Good Samaritan Hospital, 'been here almost two days. The doctor will be in to talk to ya' soon."

Jason's side and arm ached. Dejavu all over again.

"What's that bear up there?"

The nurse walked over and read the note that had been inserted in the stuffed animals paw. "Hope your troubles are over. Get well quick." It was signed Alexander (Ego).

Jason was beginning to put the pieces together.

"The flowers?"

Again the nurse read a note inserted in a bouquet. "This is a memory bouquet. We need to talk. Love, Greta."

"Ya have some nice friends and there were a few people in to see you. I guess ya don't remember."

"Who?" Jason asked, trying to put things together.

"Well, some suits came in yesterday. Real serious types. And a Marshall is outside your door checking visitors."

Jason's thinking was still muddy.

"And a soldier."

"Soldier?" he responded.

"Well...I guess ya call him a marine. Lookin' real good in his starched uniform. I have a boy 'bout his age, maybe a little younger. Studyin' to be a newspaper writer at U. of O. A good boy."

"What about the soldier...er, the marine. What did he say?"

"Just wanted to look at your face. Said he wanted to see your face."

Jason paused, puzzled, remembering Brensen. But why would he be here to look at Jason?

"Supposed he saw a white face before. Didn't say much. Reminded me of my son. Real respectful."

"What do you mean white face?"

"Well, I mean since he was black and all."

A black marine? Looking at his face? Jason was anxious and confused. He couldn't put the pieces together and felt a loss of control.

At this point the floor nurse came in to give him an injection. "Good morning Mr. Knox. Good to see you awake. Your vital signs are looking good and the doctor will be in to see you later today. Roll over please. This is just something for pain." She injected a powerful narcotic and as Jason started to ask her questions, Paul Howieson made his appearance at the door.

"Just a few minutes now. He needs to rest and the medicine will take effect shortly," bellowed the nurse. She was clearly in charge in this arena.

"Hello Jason. Good to see you."

"Hello, Paul." "What happened? Why am I here? And who is this black marine? Am I dreaming?"

"No. The marine is the sharpshooter who saved your life. From Delta Force. He belongs to the Force

Reconnaissance Assault Platoon. A highly trained commando team of the 24th Marine Expeditionary Unit. Among other 'tools' he used a night sniper scope. Somebody thought we needed backup. You'll learn who later. He's back with his unit now, but you'll get to meet him again. He just wanted to see the face of the man he saved?"

"Saved? What? How?"

"Well, it's a long story and we'll tell you more as time goes on. Sergeant Barnes, the marine, was stationed in the parking structure across from the Chinese columns. He was dressed in a parking lot attendant's uniform. He's a sharpshooter and took out your assailant. It took courage on his part to shoot and he'll be getting a military decoration at the same time you receive the Intelligence Medal. All very quietly of course. The Director wants to meet with you personally."

Paul could see that Jason was becoming restless.

He was more confused than ever. This was too much too fast. He didn't know what to ask next.

"The Chinese tried to kill me?"

"No, the French."

Now this was really too much for Jason to assimilate.

Paul explained. "There has been a deep cover French espionage operation in the Northwest for about ten years. Some of their agents work at local factories and the steel mill here in Portland. They're on extended visas and rotate every year or so. We can't penetrate them and wiretaps and surveillance have been zip. They moved in on the Chinese-Israeli operation and decided to kill you, get what they could and bust the conduit to China. If they couldn't get what they wanted no one else was going to either. We think the Israeli's ransacked your office and condo, but the French sabotaged your car. The sooner you were out of the picture the better. One less link. I can tell you you're out of danger now. This is over, at least as far as you're concerned."

"Did you make arrests? Are there witnesses?"

"No. It's not that easy in this business. The guy who tried to kill Susan is dead along with the agent who shot you. Thanks to the marine."

Jason remembered Susan. She was behind him.

"Oh God, how is she?"

"She's doing well. Be in to see you later today or maybe tomorrow."

"The case, the operation. Was it a success?" asked Jason.

"Well...I guess you could say that. We intercepted the leaks at *Letni*. No arrests though. The brains there, the computer and math types, will be reassigned elsewhere to less sensitive jobs. We learned a little about the French and have a lead on the Mossad operations in the area. All of this will be hushed up. Politics you know. As far as Portland P.D. is concerned this was a city mugging. Nothing out of the ordinary late at night in a rough part of town. Just routine. The Director already spoke with the Chief and it's all taken care of. The papers won't get the scoop and this will hardly be reported. Maybe last page in *The Oregonian*."

"Just routine?" responded Jason. "I've gone thru hell, my practice has been on hold, my personal life down the drain and I'm almost killed!"

"Don't get excited. You're a hero. You and I and a few others know what you've done. Life is short anyway. You can pick up the pieces. My job goes on. This will not end for us."

At this point the charge nurse looked in. "It's time for you to leave, please. Doctor's orders."

"There's more to tell, Jason, and I'll fill in the details tomorrow. Anything you need? Magazines, candy, hero sandwiches?" Paul was trying to be polite.

"No thanks. I wish you could stay a while longer."

At this point the phone rang and Paul handed it to Jason as he quietly slipped out of the room.

"Hello! Greta, is that you?"

"Hi, Jason, how are you? I miss you!"

"I miss you to. I can't believe what's happened. I'm all confused."

"Don't worry. I'll come to Portland in a day or two and when you're discharged. I'll drive you here to Central Oregon to recuperate. My parents have plenty of room and the air here is crisp and clean. Just what the doctor ordered."

Jason began to tell Greta about the events of the past few days, the marine sharpshooter, the F.B.I, Susan and everything he could think of.

"I know about all of that Jason. You just rest. When you're feeling better maybe we can go to D.C. together."

"D.C.?"

"Yes...the Chairman of the Senate Foreign Relations Committee wants to have us in for dinner at his home in Georgetown. He knows all about you and wants to meet you in person. He's an old school friend of my fathers. You'll...Jason?"

Before Greta could finish her sentence the narcotic had taken effect and Jason was off in a dream world. He was in high desert country. The snowflakes were falling around him, as he lay wrapped in warm blankets safe and secure from the cold outside.

Additional books by Ronald Turco, M.D.

The Architecture of Creativity
Profiles Behind the Mask

ISBN 0-9700131-2-4
$16.95

Poignantly exploring the lives of Andrew Wyeth, Duke Ellington, Mark Rothko, Yukio Mishima, Helen Hardin, Edvard Munch, Vincent VanGogh, and finally, Leonardo da Vinci, author Ronald Turco immerses us in the common thread of shared human creative experience--experience that resonates with our own lives and hidden creative processes--dormant since childhood. The stories of these artists are OUR stories. We identify with their loss, tragedy, pleasure and aspirations. Art becomes life in the truest sense--the representational and vibrant depiction of human emotion. Sensuality in its complete manifestation resonating with our own creative desires buried through time and filtered by the commonality of daily survival.

Closely Watched Shadows

ISBN 0-9700131-1-6
$14.95

A profile of the hunter and the hunted, Closely Watched Shadows is a fascinating story of forensic detection combined with the deductive thoughts of the physician/ police officer who recreated the dark personality and evil genus of a serial murderer, leading to his apprehension.

When a psychiatrist who is also a police officer is asked to join a murder task force, looking for a child serial killer, he embarks on a journey that challenges his personal integrity, values and sense of self. Turco, described on 48 Hours as an intuitive dective of the mind, embarks on a spiritual journey as he attempts to track down the perpetrator.

Books by Dr. Turco may be purchased at your local
bookseller
or ordered directly from IMAGO Books

IMAGO BOOKS
PO Box 25097
Portland, OR 97298

Phone: 503-803-4373
Fax orders to: 503-644-9775
Email orders to: 104676.1410@compuserve.com